Fleeing the Nest

BY

JUDITH BURTON WALTER

Kelly —
Judy tho't this
Vicarious escape
might be in order
at the end of 2020!
Enjoy —
Judith

This is a work of fiction. Names, characters, places, and incidents are either the product of the author's imagination or are used fictitiously.

ISBN: 1482384221
ISBN 13: 9781482384222

ACKNOWLEDGEMENTS

There are many people to acknowledge and thank for helping me finish this novel:

My co-editors, Brian and Heather Harville;

Laurie Michaud-Kay, for designing the cover;

My friends, readers, and writing mentors—particularly Sally Lee, Mary Ann Weakley, Laurie Michaud-Kay, Ginger Manley, and Louise Colln. Your hours of reading, editing, and encouraging are so greatly appreciated.

The Saturday Morning Critique Group of Franklin, TN. You encourage and critique new writers with a great deal of kindness. Thank you for that.

And my husband and daughter for their patience and encouragement, while I spent many hours at the computer.

Thank you one and all.

Judith Burton Walter

This book is dedicated to my Aunt Jessie, who inspires us all—and makes sure we put our commas in the right places. Jessie, if there are any misplaced commas in here, I take full responsibility for them!

PROLOGUE

Even I get pissed off eventually. My daughter, Mandy, popped in for dinner the night before my friend and I ran away from home. Once again, she came with my two grandchildren in tow and left as soon as dinner was over. She'd been treating me like her personal servant for years and I was fed up. On the way back from taking the kids home and waiting for Mandy to return, I decided the next day would be a good time to put an adult behavior modification plan into action. I was through being her doormat.

I called my old friend Becky the minute I got home. She had daughter issues too. Her daughter, Sonya, hovered over her and nagged about her health. That did not sit well. Becky was sixty-seven years old and not going to live forever. And if Sonya kept harping at her, she wasn't going to 'live' at all.

She answered on the second ring. "Hi, Linda. I tried to call you about an hour ago."

" I'm sure you can guess where I've been."

"I thought I saw them at your house." Becky always watched the comings and goings at my house through her front window.

"You did, but Mandy got up and left as soon as she ate. So the kids and I cleaned up here and went to their house to do homework. Mandy came strolling in about 10:00, with no explanation. I have had it. I am through letting her take advantage of me."

"Well, bravo, Linda. It's about time."

"I say we take off on a little vacation early tomorrow morning and teach both our children a lesson or two. What do you say?"

"I say what time shall I be at your house?"

"Be here at 10:00. That's enough time for us to make some food for the road and we'll get out of town without anyone having the slightest idea what's going on."

"I'll be there. This is going to be fun—two rowdy, ticked off grandmothers on the loose. You bring some Black Jack and I'll bring Beefeaters. Might as well indulge ourselves along the way." I could imagine Becky dancing in place at the thought of a new adventure.

At 9:45 the next morning, after packing and making some picnic food, I glanced out the window and saw Becky pulling her luggage and a cooler across the street. Lord, I hoped she wasn't planning to drink that much Beefeaters. I opened the garage door and called to her, "I'm thinking you want to take my car—or do you plan on walking?"

"Geeze. Am I going to have to listen to your smart mouth for this whole trip? Of course, I want to take your car."

I always drove when the two of us went places. I liked to be in control and Becky liked to give directions without taking responsibility for them.

We met at the back of my car, heaved our bags into the trunk, and put the cooler in the back seat. I eased out of my driveway and gunned it when we got to the main highway.

chapter

ONE

Becky and I left home with no warning to our children, no planning, and very little money. I didn't intend to stop that first day except to eat and pee—and not necessarily in that order. We needed to put some miles between us and the people who might, or might not, be looking for us.

At noon, after only one pit stop earlier, I pulled off the interstate and drove by a park in the small town we entered. The grass was mowed, flowers bloomed, and children played in the playground. It looked welcoming, so I slowed up.

Becky perked up. "Let's stop here and have lunch." She was always hungry. Probably how she wound up being a little plump.

"Only if they have a toilet available. I need to go again."

"My God, Linda. Do you have a pipe straight through you?"

"Oh, shut up. I see a parking area and a building up ahead. I'm going over there."

I swung the Toyota into a parking spot and pulled myself out of the car. My body crunched and creaked when I moved and the gravel walkway echoed in response. Not everything about age sixty-seven was fun.

Rounding a half wall that blocked my view, I got quite a shock. No wonder they wanted to block the view. I had wandered into the men's locker room and there stood a dozen old men with their bare behinds right in front of me. I stood frozen in place. My view gave a whole new meaning to bagging and sagging.

I tried to back out without being noticed, but Becky yelled a moment too late. I backed into an old metal trashcan at the exit—which I had used for an entrance—and my quiet retreat came to an abrupt end. The trashcan banged and clanged all the way down the walk to the corner of the building and I landed in the grass on my backside right in view of the 'Senior Chippendales'. Every man in the locker room turned in unison to see what the ruckus was about.

I threw up my hand and smiled. "Looking good, boys. Looking good." They couldn't decide whether to strut their stuff or limit their exposure. I pulled myself up and hurried back to the car, trying to get away before I got hysterical.

Becky already had tears rolling down her cheeks and she hadn't even seen the Senior Chippendales. I slammed the car door and leaned on the steering wheel, laughing too hard to breathe. After I got control and finished gasping for breath, I started the car and drove to the clearly marked public bathrooms on the other side of the park.

By then I could speak again. "Well, I've had my thrill for the day. I wish you could have seen those old geezers. Makes me glad I live alone. Let's wash up and find a picnic table. There has to be one somewhere—away from the pool."

Becky got out the signs of her clean hands fetish—her own soap, towel, Lysol wipes and a pair of latex gloves. She had not always been this way, but for the last few years she drove me crazy on the whole subject of public bathrooms and clean hands. Fortunately, she didn't worry as much about her dirty mind and that kept things interesting, if somewhat neurotic.

On our way back to the car, we saw a picnic table. Each of us retrieved a food container from the back seat of the car and put everything on the weathered and splintery wooden table, which was polka-dotted with bird droppings. I hoped Becky would not have to clean that too. I put the cooler over the worst of it and opened up the plastic containers of food in a hurry, hoping the scent of food would help avoid that whole scenario. It worked. After loading up our Dixie plates, we plopped down with a sigh of relief. It felt good to be out of the car and not worried with traffic.

Holding a fried chicken leg in mid-air, Becky reminded me how she loved my cooking. "Linda, I swear you make the best fried chicken east of the Mississippi."

"Thanks. I can't wait to get into that Coca Cola cake of yours. It's my favorite dessert in the world. I can't believe you had time to make one."

"There's plenty of it."

We continued our lunch in silence, thinking about the children and grandchildren we happily left behind.

Becky spoke first. "You know, I haven't enjoyed a meal this much in I can't remember when. Sonya would be preaching about cholesterol and exercise about now and ruining it all." Then she asked the question she'd been avoiding all morning. "Speaking of her, do you think we should get our cell phones and call the kids before we leave here? Or at least check for messages?"

"Absolutely not. We can't teach them a lesson by checking in every five minutes. I say we don't call until at least tomorrow night." I hated cell phones. I didn't want to stay connected all the time. Being on call for so many years as a social worker took the pleasure out of that proposition.

"You don't think Sonya will send the cops looking for us?"

I shrugged my shoulders. "So what if she does? By the time they could find us, we will have called home. And anyway, is there a law against two old friends having some fun?"

"You're right. Anyway, I confess I left a note for Sonya telling her we were taking a trip. She'll use her key and find it before the day's over. So where are we headed from here?"

"Let's get on the interstate and keep going west. We'll stop when it begins to get dark."

"Sounds like a plan. Are you ready to get on the road again?"

"Hey, that can be our theme song for this trip." I began a loud version of that old Willie Nelson hit and Becky got up and moving.

"My God! You sound like a moose with congestion."

I chuckled. "Thank you for that appraisal of my talents. My feelings are hurt, you old goat."

I don't know when Becky and I began being so sarcastic with each other, but it was a permanent part of our friendship. Since my retirement, I added a bit of a salty vocabulary to the sarcasm. So many years of containing myself with clients made me take pleasure in letting it rip now. Becky had always let it rip.

We left the park and hit the road singing. When it began to get dark, I watched for the next exit. My night vision was none too good and by this time, there were probably three hundred miles between home and us.

"I'm gonna get off at the next exit. You watch for a place to stay. Should we eat in our room and finish the lunch leftovers?"

"I guess so. I'm glad you're getting off the interstate. Everybody wants you to go over the speed limit. I'm tired of all those people honking at us and having to shoot 'em a bird. My hand's tired."

"I can only imagine." I had to smile at her spunkiness. And hoped we wouldn't be the victims of road rage. "Now, watch for a motel. A cheap one. We're going to have to figure out our finances tonight and make a plan. I don't have much cash."

A few miles off the interstate, Becky slapped my arm. "Hey, slow down. I think I saw a Motel 6 sign. Let me get my other glasses—I can't read the sign with these." Becky fumbled around in the glove box and found the extra glasses she had stashed in there. Squinting and straining her neck forward, she confirmed the Motel 6 just ahead.

I was grateful it was on the right; I didn't make left turns, since I'd been broadsided a year earlier—and it was not my fault, regardless of what the cops said.

I maneuvered into the parking lot and Becky went in with her credit card. I watched her walk across the parking lot. She still had a straight back and lengthy stride. Even though her short hair was graying, she didn't look her age. Her figure fell somewhere between shapely and plump and her flawless skin made her look younger than her sixty-seven years. We were both lucky that way, and I knew Becky would make the most of that.

Then my mind turned to more practical things. I was a planner, and one thing I knew about my cash—I only had enough to gas up the car from time to time. We really did need a plan and some more money.

Becky came out waving a key and pointing to the other side of the building. Our room was around the corner on the first floor. She opened the door, but I waited to go in. "Check it out and see if it's clean enough for us."

She poked her head in the bathroom and pulled the bedding back to see if there was any sign of bed bugs. The room showed signs of wear, but it seemed to be clean and had two beds.

"This will do," she announced.

A sign of relief escaped before I could stop it. I didn't think I could sleep with the smell of Lysol. Once everything was inside, we each fell across a bed. After a few minutes, I bunched up the pillows and sat up with my legs stretched out. Leaning against what passed for a headboard made even me a little squeamish about other people's dirt.

"Okay. Let's figure out how to handle the money."

Becky propped herself up on one elbow and looked at me. "How much do you have?"

"I have two hundred dollars, but that won't go far. How much can you afford to put on your credit card?"

"I think I shouldn't put more than five hundred dollars on it. I can pay that when we go home, but I'd have to dip into my IRA for more than that. Of course, we'll have it for any emergency."

"How much did this room cost?"

"About thirty dollars, I think."

"Geeze—didn't you ask?"

"What difference would it make? We were gonna stop anyway." She shrugged her shoulders. "So if we spend $30.00 a day for a room and $30.00 a day for food, we can be gone for at least a week. But that's not enough time to teach the girls much."

"Not enough money either. You obviously haven't looked at the price side of a menu in a while. Maybe we should have waited until *after* our social security checks came."

"Oh, don't be a killjoy. It wouldn't have been near as much fun without the running away from home part. We'll figure out something. Let's eat our leftovers and watch some TV."

While Becky filled our plates, I checked my cell phone for messages. "Well, well. Mandy called. Let's see what she has to say. She must need something." I put it on speakerphone and laid it on the dresser.

Mandy's voice sounded strained. "Mom, when you get this message, call me."

Her belated concern didn't impress me. "A little worry is good for people, don't you think?"

"What I think is that you said you weren't going to check in until tomorrow."

"I'm not going to call her. I just wanted to see if she had called me."

Becky chuckled. "Are you sure you don't want to call? After all, we may have to ask her for money and I'd rather she was speaking to you when we do."

We both smiled at that thought. Mandy had a good job, but hell would freeze over before I asked her for help. After all, my goal was to teach her independence and asking for money would be what she would do—not me.

Becky turned on the TV, handed me my supper, and we settled in for the night. I brought out my Jack Daniels when she got her Beefeaters and, by the time the ten o'clock news came on, we were both a little giggly.

I saw Becky nodding and turned the TV off. "I think we'd better turn in. Tomorrow we'll make some plans for money. Maybe we can get creative about making a few bucks." I didn't know if that was optimism or Jack Daniels talking.

"Making a few bucks sounds good to me." Becky smirked and I knew she did not mean money. Our finances might have to include separate rooms.

***

Driving out of the parking lot the next morning, I realized getting on the interstate required left turns and merging. I decided against that.

"Let's take the state roads. They're more interesting and maybe no one will honk at us for driving the speed limit. We'll stop for breakfast at the first decent place we come to. The eateries around here don't look too promising."

"Sounds good to me. Let's go."

I turned right onto the highway and sped up. Becky found the glasses she needed to read signs and began watching for a place to eat.

"Now, remember. I don't make left turns without a left turn arrow. Find us a place on the right."

"Well, hell Linda. What if there aren't any places on the right? Are we just going to starve? Don't be such a wuss."

"Well, who wouldn't take their car and be the driver, Miss Know-it-all?"

"Okay. I'll look on the right—for a while." In a mile or so, Becky slapped my arm and pointed ahead. "Hey, there's a Country Rocker restaurant and it's on the right." She turned toward me with a grin. "I always wanted to be a country rocker and I think this restaurant is as close as I'll get."

"I think you're right about that. Now, help me see the driveway. Sometimes I can't watch the road and find a driveway at the same time. God, are we getting old, Becky?"

"Absolutely not. Your eyesight's not so good though. Maybe I should take a turn driving after breakfast."

"Not in my lifetime. You couldn't drive worth a damn when you were young."

Inside the restaurant, a perky waitress who personified the phrase "more bounce to the ounce," sashayed across the dining room to direct us to a seat.

"Will this be okay?" the waitress drawled, pointing to a window table for two.

Becky answered for us. "Sure. Any place is fine."

"So, what do you want to do today?" I asked, as the waitress poured our coffee.

"Let's just drive west and see what turns up. Maybe we'll meet some hot cowboys."

"Becky, I'm not sure we'd remember what to do with hot cowboys."

"Oh, we'd remember." She wiggled her eyebrows for emphasis.

Our food arrived and the conversation ended. We might not focus on some things as well as we used to, but we could still focus on our food like a laser beam.

In a few minutes, Becky sopped up the last drop of gravy with her biscuit. "Hmmm. That was good. Now let's do a little planning about the girls. What do you want to teach Mandy?"

I raised my eyebrows. "I thought we weren't going to plan anymore?"

"Oh, don't be a smartass."

I thought for a moment before answering. "I'm not sure exactly what I want to accomplish with this trip as far as Mandy goes. Maybe I just need a break from the ugliness. I do know I brought the Yellow Pages with me and every time she mentions something I do for her, I'm going to call and find out what it would cost her to pay someone to do it. When the time's right, I'm gonna' tell her what I'm worth." I paused before continuing. "Maybe what I want is for her to 'get it' that she depends on me way too much and appreciates me way too little."

"And when you get home, are you prepared to force that issue of her dependence on you? She is way too into the idea of 'Ask and ye shall receive'."

"Good Lord, Becky. When did you begin spouting off scripture?"

"I haven't. It just seemed to fit the situation. But you need to be able to enjoy your retirement and not keep taking on Mandy's responsibilities."

"I know. It's just easier to do things than experience her rage sometimes."

"I don't understand her attitude. You've been a great mother." Becky shook her head. "I don't understand her."

We were quiet for a while. When the waitress freshened up our coffee, Becky continued, as she stirred her coffee. "When did her ugliness start?"

"Right after George died. She adored her father, and I think it all started when she only heard half of something I said."

"What are you talking about?" For once, Becky looked bewildered.

"I've never told anyone this." I hesitated and fortified myself with a drink of fresh, hot coffee. "Mandy and I were out walking one day after her Dad died. She said how guilty she felt for not spending more time with him. I said that I had some of the same thoughts and was disgusted with myself, because I knew I'd been a good wife. Mandy didn't hear anything past '...I'm disgusted'. She thought, and still thinks, I meant I was disgusted with her. Nothing I've ever said or done convinces her differently. I guess I've been trying to serve or buy my way back into her heart since then."

"Oh, Linda. That makes me so sad. Why didn't you ever talk to me about that?"

"I don't know. I guess I felt stupid for getting myself into that spot." I looked down and flicked a crumb off the table before continuing. " Now, let's talk about Sonya. Do you have a plan of action there?"

"Not really. She's a great daughter, but she is driving me crazy about my health. She nags all the time and I feel like I live under her personal microscope." She looked at me with unusual seriousness. "Do you have any suggestions?"

"Maybe just tell her the truth— you're going to die from her nagging a lot quicker than from your cholesterol."

"Like she'd believe that."

Getting more serious, I thought aloud. "Maybe she'll get it by us being away by ourselves for a while and surviving without her health reminders. She does need to get a grip about the aging process. She can't keep you alive forever."

"Well, that's just what I needed to hear." She rolled her eyes in dismay.

"You know what I mean."

"Yeah. Let's get going. I'm sure we'll come back to this topic many times. Right now, let's go have ourselves an adventure. We haven't had a real adventure since we became widows. It's long overdue."

"I agree."

As I put the key in the ignition, I noted, "I need to get some gas. Watch for a place on the right."

Within a mile, Becky pointed to the left toward an old Phillips 66 station. I got brave and turned on my left blinker and waited for oncoming traffic to clear. After all it was mid-morning and a state road. How hard could it be?

Pulling up to the pump, an old geezer came outside. He looked older than the station. I put the window down just as he reached the car.

"Mornin' ma'am. What can I do for you?" He peered inside the car to get a good look.

"Fill it up, please."

He sauntered toward the back of the car. I turned toward Becky, with a look of astonishment. "I can't believe he's pumping gas for us." When the tank was full, he screwed on the cap and walked back to my open window.

He opened his eyes wider and smiled, which rearranged his wrinkles and displayed two rows of discolored, overlapping teeth. "Can I do anything else for you, honey? You're a long way from home."

"Nothing else, thank you." I handed him the exact amount the pump said I owed him and put the window up. Becky was about to have one of her laughing fits by the time I got back on the road.

"I think that old geezer was flirting with you."

"Well, I hope I can do better than that."

"Maybe. Maybe not."

"Well, if I can't do better than that I'll just keep doing without, thank you."

Becky guffawed and we were off and running.

chapter

TWO

We drove through the flatlands of west Tennessee, and by noon, we were somewhere in Missouri on US 64 West. Farms and small towns glided by the windows and sometimes bumped by, depending on the road conditions. I wasn't sure I'd want to live in the area, but it might prove interesting to visit.

Becky must have had the same thought. "Let's stop in the next town we come to—it's not like we're going to come to a large city."

"I think we need to get a map so we know how close we are to things. We may run through this whole tank of gas before we find a town."

"Oh, don't be silly. We'll find one soon."

She was right. In less than an hour, I drove into a town that looked a lot like the place where we grew up in Tennessee. Going around the square—going *around* a square always sounded odd to me—I spotted a diner called the City Café.

"Let's go there for lunch. I'll bet it's a good meat-and-three."

"You're the driver. And I'm easy to get along with, you know."

"Yeah. Right," I chuckled inwardly.

I parked three slots down from the diner. We got out, stretched our legs, and leaned left and right to ease the kinks in our backs.

"Let's walk around the square before we go in. We could use some exercise. It might rev up our metabolism." Becky tried to stay curvy rather than chunky.

We passed a shop with a window full of photographs of the local countryside and some exotic shots of the Ozark Mountains. A sign over the door identified it as "The Framery." Next door, we saw a hardware store, with every conceivable gadget needed on a farm or in a house. We continued around the square and the last two shops on the circle were a small bakery and a seamstress shop. A typical small town square.

After looking around the square again, I asked, "Do you remember when our town square had one side filled with beer joints? The church people called that the Devil's Elbow."

"Yeah. I didn't understand that then, and I still don't. I'd love a cold beer right now. Wonder if the City Café sells beer?"

"What do you think, Becky? We're in small town rural America."

As we approached our car, a cop was looking at the car and license. "Oh, shit. I wonder what he's looking for. Or who."

Becky looked over her glasses and then at me. "I'll bet Sonya has them looking for us. Damn, I wish she would just give me a little credit."

We took our time walking those last few feet. "Good morning, officer. Can I help you? That's my car you're looking at."

"Just checking the license plate. It's awful close to one posted at the office. Somebody we're looking for."

"Oh, sir. We're just a couple of old friends on a road trip. You must be looking for someone else. Would you like to see my license and registration?"

"Oh, that's okay. You two couldn't possibly be who I'm looking for. Ya'll have a nice day." He tipped his hat and walked away.

Becky looked over her glasses again. "Well, I think I'll have to clean my shoes, from standing in all that bullshit."

"You'd better be glad I'm quick witted. Now let's go get some lunch."

A chubby middle-aged man greeted us inside the cafe. He grabbed two greasy menus before showing us to a table.

"What would you ladies like to drink?"

Being true to our heritage, we ordered sweet tea.

Becky watched him go to the counter for our drinks. "Tubby could use a few walks around the square himself."

"Hush, Becky. He'll hear you."

"Well, we don't know him. What difference does it make? It's the truth."

"Be nice. I saw a help wanted sign in the window. What do you think of applying for a job?"

"That's not a bad idea. Where would we stay?"

"Maybe 'Tubby'—if you haven't offended him—can make a suggestion."

Our tea arrived, and the gentleman in question decided to introduce himself. "Glad you ladies stopped by. My name's Tubby. Where you folks from?"

I thought I would spit my tea right on him. Neither Becky nor I could speak. Tubby frowned, looked at us as if we were nuts, and went back to the front of the café.

Becky summed it up. "Well—so much for applying for the job."

***

After lunch, we decided to drive around and see what this little town looked like away from the square. I looked over at Becky and made a suggestion. "Maybe we should stay here a few weeks and try to find some work. That way we can stretch our dollars."

"What on earth could we do? And what if that deputy comes back looking for us?"

"Oh, I can handle that deputy. We've been slinging hash for our families our whole adult lives. Why can't we do that with a little pizzazz at the City Café and make some tip money, if Tubby will hire us?"

"Well, I've got the pizzazz. I'm not so sure about you though."

"Excuse me. I have my own brand of pizzazz."

We approached an antique store on our right, and I decided to stop and take a look around.

"Why are we stopping here?" Becky's interest in old things only extended as far as old men.

"Thought we might ask a few questions about jobs and who knows—maybe we'll find a painting for five dollars that's worth millions."

"Dream on, sister. Dream on."

The antique store smelled of dust, mold, furniture polish, and air fresheners. That sometimes meant bargains. As we walked around, we picked up familiar patterns of glassware, and I looked at all the paintings for signatures I might recognize. Becky inspected furniture.

A woman near our age walked over and asked if she could help us.

"Not right now. Maybe later." I smiled at the woman.

"Well, just give me a yell if you need something." She walked away, but stayed close enough to watch us. I guess she figured a stranger would be either a good customer or a shoplifter, and she wasn't taking any chances on us.

After wandering around the shop, I walked over where the woman stood. Up close, she looked a few years younger than we did and my gut told me she was a pleasant person, in spite of the watchfulness. "We're on a road trip and stopping in interesting places. We thought we might stay here for a few days."

"I think you'd like it. It's quiet, but I like living here." She looked up from her dusting.

"We're looking for a place to stay and maybe a part-time job while we're here. Do you know anybody who might need some help for a few days?"

"What're you interested in?"

"Anything really. We just wanted to make a little extra money while we're here."

"Hmm. I think the drugstore had a sign in the window last time I drove by. The pharmacist's name is Doug Parman. And there are always the fast food places on the highway—they can't keep help. And I believe the City Café needs a waitress right now, while Janey is on maternity leave."

I didn't dare look at Becky, and I managed to keep a straight face. "Thanks. We'll check those out. I like your shop. Before we leave town we may come back and buy a few things." I suspected the good old boy system worked here much as it did in Millerton, in which case buttering up a local businessperson couldn't hurt.

"Well, I hope you find something. Maybe I'll see you in the next few days."

Back in the car, we decided to drive around and see the area further out of town. Just beyond the city limits, a sign caught my eye—"Wild West Saloon" in bright green neon letters. "Now that looks promising. Let's get a room somewhere and at least stay tonight and check that out. What do you think?"

"I think you're getting the hang of this letting go and having fun. Good for you, Linda. Having some fun is long overdue for us."

"I agree. Let's check out those job possibilities and then find a cheap motel. Where shall we start?"

"I think we should start with the drug store. Tubby will not want to talk to two laughing lunatics, much less hire us, and I have not sunk to flipping burgers—yet."

"Agreed. Where is the drug store? Did you see one on the square?"

"I think I saw an old Rexall sign. It's probably there."

Circling the square, we found a parking spot under the Rexall sign. Becky opened her door before I turned the engine off.

"Just stay put. I'll go in and do a little sweet talking."

I turned the engine off and waited. In less than fifteen minutes, Becky emerged from the drug store with a big smile.

"Well. What will you be doing?

"Who said I had the job?" She hated that I could read her like a book.

"The big smile on your face said it. Now give."

"I start tomorrow. They just need someone to fill in at the register in the afternoons for the next couple of weeks or so. That will be perfect."

"Alright. Let's find a room and I'll try to sweet talk the manager into a weekly rate."

There were no chain motels in this little town. We passed a couple of things—an obvious fleabag on the edge of town, a bed and breakfast that we thought would be out of our price range. Then we ran onto a local establishment called Frank's Place that might pass muster. There wasn't a single car in the parking lot.

"Okay. I'll do the talking this time. You just stay put and look pitiful."

I looked in the mirror to fluff up my grey and white bob and make sure I didn't have lipstick on my teeth. I strolled into the "lobby" and saw a man sitting off to the side reading a newspaper. He looked neither happy nor unhappy. He appeared to be very tall and thin and had a head full of dark hair. Wrinkles gave away his age, however. I guessed him to be in his late sixties.

"Hello. My friend and I are on a trip and decided to stop here for a few days. This seems like a nice little town."

"Yes, ma'am. I like it alright." He put the paper down in his lap to get a look at me.

"I'll bet you get lots of tourists stopping here."

"Nope. Everybody stays close to the interstate these days." He hadn't moved, and his expression did not change.

"What a shame! I'll be sure to tell my friends and family to come through here."

"Can I help you with something?"

"I hope so. I wondered if you had any rooms available."

I could see his eyes light up with dollar signs. He folded his paper and unfolded his long, lean frame.

"Let me look at my registery and see what we have for tonight."

Okay, I thought. I can play this game too. "I stopped at a couple of other places and didn't want to decide until I checked out your place. I hope you have a room."

" Yeah. Number 210 is available, and it's cleaned already. Would you like to see it?"

"Why, thank you. I think I would. You know, I never buy a pig in a poke."

He reached up for a key before answering. "You have to be careful these days. People always trying to rip each other off."

"I know. I'm betting you're not that way."

We walked up a short flight of steps, and he opened the second door on the right. He stood back to let me go in first. Thank God, my back was to him. Threadbare chenille bedspreads covered the beds, and the two chairs looked twenty years old with the accumulated dirt to prove it. Opening the windows would take care of the musty smell. I stuck my head around the bathroom door and almost gasped. It didn't even meet my bad standards of housekeeping. But Becky had her latex gloves, and we could buy a sponge and large bottle of Lysol.

Turning back to the manager, I flashed him my brightest smile. "This is charming. We may not be able to afford it. How much per night?"

" This one is fifty dollars a night."

"I knew it. We can't afford that. Do you have a senior citizen discount? My friend and I are seniors, and we're on what will probably be our last road trip together. We'd really like to stay here, if you could make us a good deal for a week."

I walked out into the hallway ahead of him, and he locked the door. Waiting for an answer, it was obvious he didn't share Becky's spontaneous way of making decisions. "If we can't afford it, we'll just have to go back to the last place we looked. I appreciate you showing me the room though."

"I might be able to make you a deal if you're staying for a week. How about $200 for the week? Could you handle that?"

I fished around in my purse for pen and paper and did some imaginary figuring. "Yes, we can do that. Thank you so much. I'll be sure all my friends and family know what a nice place this is and how kind you are. Could we check in right now?"

"Sure. I'll come and help you with your suitcases. They might be too heavy for you to take up those steps."

"Why, thank you. Aren't you sweet!"

Becky had a conniption when she saw the room. We had to go right out for a sponge and some Lysol and as long as we were in the grocery, we bought junk food for supper. We had plenty of dessert and libations. After cleaning the bathroom and anything else we might have to touch, Becky turned on the soap operas.

"Do you watch these things, Becky?"

"Only when I'm feeling desperate. Or a little voyeuristic."

As the heavy breathing hit a fever pitch on the TV, we both fell asleep. When I woke, I decided to look up the number for the Wild West Saloon.

A husky voice answered the phone—sounded like he might have been participating in that soap opera.

"What time do y'all open?"

"Open at 5:00. Stay open 'til about 1:00 or whenever people leave."

"Do you serve dinner?"

"Well, depends on what you call dinner. We have burgers and stuff like that. Only 'til 7:00 though."

"Okay. Thanks for the information."

Becky rolled over to face me, looking somewhat irritated that I disturbed her sleep. "Who the hell are you talking to?"

"I called the Wild West Saloon. They open at five and are open until about one the guy said. Let's go out there tonight."

"At least I could get a cold beer. My Beefeaters is not gonna last forever. And maybe there'll be dancing—you know how I love to dance."

"What time do you want to go?"

"Let's get there early enough to look the place over." She got out of bed looking happy at the prospect of a cold beer.

"You mean to look over the likely prospects, I imagine."

"That too." She couldn't suppress a giggle.

"Do you think we should call the girls before we go?"

"Maybe. It's been two days. I'll take my shower first, and you call Mandy."

Becky closed the bathroom door to give me some privacy. Mandy answered on the second ring. "Mom. Where on earth are you?" I couldn't tell if I heard anger or amazement that I had the nerve to leave home.

"Well, we're in Missouri right now. About to get ready to go dancing at the Wild West Saloon."

"I'm glad Sonya found that note and called me. I would have been worried. When are you coming home?"

"I'm not sure. We'll be home when we run out of money. That won't be for a while though 'cause Becky has a part-time job in this little town, and I'm going to look for one tomorrow."

"Well, who will take Matthew and Melinda to football and dance?" Reality was sinking in, and Mandy was, at best, whining.

"I don't know, Mandy. I'm sure you'll work it out. I saw a business in the Yellow Pages that furnishes transportation for kids whose parents are working. You might want to try them."

"And I guess they'll take care of them after school too?" The whining turned to snarling.

"I doubt it. There are people who can do that. Hazel might do it. She could probably use the extra cash."

"Well, the last two days have been a disaster. I'll be glad when you come home. The kids miss you, and I'm just chasing my tail trying to get everything done." Snarl, snarl.

I fought to keep an even tone of voice. "Mandy, the kids are your responsibility—not mine. I'll help out when I come back, but I'm not ever going back to taking care of them all the time."

"What's wrong with you? Have I offended you or something?"

"Let's have that conversation later. I just want you to know that when I come back, things are going to be different. I want some time for me and to have some fun. So as you get things arranged, you might want to make permanent arrangements."

"I get your message. I'll see you when I see you. Call me if you need anything." The buckshot of sarcasm came through the phone and sprayed me in the face.

"Why thank you, Mandy. I appreciate that. And I love you, hon'." No matter what, all our conversations ended with that. If I dropped dead as her father had, I wanted my last words to her to be that I loved her.

"You too." The phone slammed in my ear.

I breathed a sigh of relief that the first conversation was over.

Becky finished with her shower, and I went to take mine. She was waiting for an answer when I closed the door—almost. I wanted to hear their conversation.

When Sonya answered, she must have asked where we were.

"We're in Missouri somewhere. We decided to have ourselves some fun."

After a pause, Becky continued. "Yes. I've got all my medications, and I'm taking good care of myself. In fact, we're about to go dancing. That's good aerobic exercise."

Another pause, most likely filled with a tirade by Sonya. "Sonya, I am not too old to have some fun. I'm being extra careful of my health. I even promise to practice safe sex, if I meet a hot cowboy."

Lord, I wish I could have heard Sonya's response to that. I'm guessing she said something like 'I can't believe you'd do that'.

"What, you don't want me to practice safe sex? Why on earth not?" I hoped Sonya was in the mood for kidding around, even though I didn't think Becky was kidding.

"Oh. Really?" Another short pause on Becky's part. "Well, I'm not too old for that either. Get a grip Sonya."

After a few minutes of silence, she ended the conversation. "We'll come home when we run out of money or get bored—whichever happens first. I'm thinking we'll run out of money first. You take care of yourself and tell Ralph and the kids hello. I'll talk to the kids when I call in a few days. Love you. Bye."

Turning toward the bathroom, Becky shouted. "You can stop straining your ears now, Linda."

"Good. I'm getting a crick in my neck trying to hear."

chapter

THREE

At 4:30, we began to evaluate our western wardrobes. We both brought jeans—with elastic waists of course—and I was the proud owner of some lizard skin boots. We decided on tunic length tops, which would keep us cool if there was dancing. I added a gold link belt, and Becky wore a wooden bead necklace and earrings. I always opted for something to show off my hint of a waistline and Becky always opted for jewelry that would draw attention to her face.

It took a little sucking in and bolstering up, but we looked good when we left. I hoped I could find the Wild West Saloon again. My sense of direction might not be so good, but I felt my sense of adventure growing.

Going into the Wild West Saloon was like time travel to the forbidden places of our youth. I even felt a little guilty when I went in. Fortunately, that didn't last long. You could smell stale cigar smoke and beer. There was minimal light, and the grease from the kitchen hung in the air. Mixing with the cigar smoke and beer, it created a distinctive odor. The place was filled with all ages, shapes, and sizes. Of course, at first I didn't realize that. It was so dark I couldn't see a thing for several minutes.

"Becky, I can't see a thing. I'll just follow you, and you tell me when I can sit down. Find a good table for us."

"Okay. Follow me. I think we'll sit at the bar." She made sure she stayed only a couple of steps ahead of me. After a brief walk to our right and bumping into several barstools, Becky stopped. She discreetly turned me a bit to the left and told me to sit down. I started to do exactly that.

"Well, hello little lady." That was not Becky's voice.

When I felt a hand on my ass, I knew I was about to sit in someone's lap. Apparently, Becky didn't understand the concept of 'I can't see in the dark.'

"Excuse me! My eyes haven't adjusted to the dark, and my friend told me to sit down. I guess she didn't mean here."

"Oh, that's fine, honey. You just go right ahead and have a seat."

Moving his hand, I switched to my don't-mess-with-me voice. "I don't think so." By now, my eyes had adjusted to the dim light, and I saw Becky two seats down doubled over laughing. I will pay her back, I thought. I moved down the way with as much dignity as I could muster under the circumstances.

"Becky, the next time we go somewhere this dark, I'll just stand at the entrance until my eyes adjust. What were you thinking when you told me to sit down?"

"I was thinking you would walk to the bar stool two steps in front of you. I didn't think you'd sit in the one right behind you. Lord, can't you see anything?"

"Not when I go from a lighted parking lot to a dark saloon. It takes a few minutes."

I looked back to where I first sat. He wasn't so bad—ten-gallon hat, boots hooked over the rungs of the bar stool, and well built. *Hmm. Maybe I'll go back and sit there after all.* He nodded toward me, tipped his hat, and raised a beer in salute. A lecherous smile flitted across his mouth.

I nodded in response and turned my back to him. The bartender walked over, and we ordered a Bud Light and sat back to size the place up. There was a table across the way full of young women on the prowl. They scoped out the place and made behind-the-hands remarks to each other. A few feet from them, there was a table with an equal number of roving male eyes. Closer to the door, three middle-aged women sat, trying to cover their awkwardness with forced smiles and occasional laughter.

"I don't know, Becky. This looks like a pretty raunchy place."

"Just what we need. We won't stay late. That way when it gets rowdy we'll be gone. Sit back and enjoy."

The bartender brought our beers and slid them across the wide oak bar. "Where you ladies from?" he asked as he continued to mix drinks for people.

"Oh, we're just passing through. Thought we'd check out the night life." Becky could talk to anybody at any given moment.

"Well, you're looking it. This is our night life."

"Do you live here?" I asked.

"I'm from around here. Won't be for long though. I'm earning some money for college next semester. What are two nice ladies like you doing in here by yourself?"

"Oh, like she said, we're on a cross country trip and just stopping here and there. Decided to stay here a few days."

"Why?"

"Why did we stop or why did we come here?"

He smiled at that question. "Both."

"Actually, we needed to stop and make a little money."

I was glad when Becky took the conversation back. "I'm going to be working at the drugstore for the next week or two. We came here to have some fun before I go to work."

I nodded my head toward the man I encountered coming in. "Who's the guy to my right?"

The bartender looked down the bar and smiled. "Oh, that's Earl. He's in here every night. Always trying to pick up a woman and never quite succeeding."

Oops, I thought. *I'll have to keep my eye on him. Not a lap to sit in.* My sense of adventure had not grown that much.

As the night progressed, the decibels rose in direct relationship to the amount of beer served. By 8 o'clock, the voices were loud and so was the frequent laughter. From time to time, there was a cowboy whoop from some macho male on the prowl. We talked to several people at the bar. Most were men, but there were a couple of tough looking females too.

I leaned over toward Becky so people couldn't hear me and said, "Let's move to a table, Becky. The bar doesn't attract the best of the crowd."

"Oh, you are such a prissy old woman. Okay. Can you see where you're going this time?"

"I'll lead the way. Just follow me."

I noticed two nice looking gentlemen eyeing us from a corner table. I made my way over to sit near them. If there was going to be dancing, I would rather be there than at the bar.

We put our beer and purses down and settled into more comfortable chairs. I looked at the corner table. One man was easy on the eyes—tall, thin, with graying hair. The other one was balding and had a bit of a paunch. I elbowed Becky and asked, "What do you think of those two sitting in the corner?"

She turned to take a look. "Good Lord. One of them is the druggist."

"Which one?"

"The one with the paunch. Why?"

"I like the look of the other one."

Shortly, the canned music stopped and someone with a microphone announced that line dancing lessons would begin in fifteen minutes.

"What fun! Have you ever done any line dancing, Linda?"

"Not in a long time. Maybe I can relearn it. One thing is for sure, I have to find the bathroom first. I've had three beers and you know how that goes."

She laughed. "Yea. Straight through you."

I wound through the tables to the back where spotlights were shining on the doors to the facilities. The faint odor of cleaner told me it might be clean enough even for Becky. The line was long and, while we waited, some of us began doing our own version of line dancing. By the time I got back to the table, the real line dancing was about to begin.

"You really think we ought to try this?"

Becky didn't hesitate. "Sure. If we make a fool of ourselves, we'll never see any of these people again, so it doesn't matter. Come on."

We lined up with about thirty other people. I noticed the table of middle-aged women did not join the group. The guy with the microphone was the nice looking one from the corner table.

"Ready everybody? How many of you have ever done any line dancing?"

Most of the hands went up. Mine were noticeably down at my side.

"I'll go slow for those who haven't done this before. Anybody want to volunteer to help me demonstrate the steps?"

The floosies raised their hands, but the guy looked straight at me. "How about you little lady? Come on up here, and I'll give you a private lesson." He wiggled his eyebrows to the 'audience' and applause broke out.

Oh dear, I thought. *How did I get myself in this mess?*

"What's your name little lady?" he asked as he took my hand to help me up the steps.

"First of all, I am not little and some would say not a lady. But my name is Linda."

"Alright. I guess you put me in my place, Linda. My name is Jake—Jake Dotson. Let's dance."

The twangy country music cranked up and the dance steps, thank God, came back to me. I was touching, tapping, brushing, and doing left and right vines all over the place. I even managed to pivot a few times. Heaven help us, I had let a genie out of a bottle, and I had a feeling that bottle might never get corked again. This whole scene was more fun than I had had in a long time.

During the first break, Becky told me she thought we should leave. I couldn't believe my ears. "Why? It's still early, and they're going to be dancing some more."

"I know, but I've got to go."

"Well, there's a ladies room right back there. Go."

"I don't mean that. I have got to GO." She spoke low and slow, and I knew that meant business.

"Well, let me say good night to the instructor. He was pretty nice. I'll be right back."

I found the dance teacher and thanked him for refreshing my dance memory.

"I hope I see you here again. I teach dance once a week. Come back." His genuine smile was more to my liking than the smirk I saw earlier.

"Maybe I'll see you next week. Thanks again."

Going out, I noticed that Becky was walking funny. Maybe somebody stepped on her foot while she was dancing. Or maybe it was just hard to walk on the gravel parking lot. When we were out of earshot of the guys standing around outside, I finally asked what the problem was.

"My God. You will not believe it. When I started back to the table at break, I felt it start, and I knew I had to get out of there in a hurry."

"What are you talking about?" I was sure she hadn't started her period, so I had no idea what she was talking about.

"I felt something moving on my inner thighs. I couldn't squish it or shake it loose so I knew it was not a bug. Then I remembered what that feeling was. One of my thigh highs was creeping down and they don't stop until they are around my ankles. I'm lucky I got out of there before that happened. I figured if I walked stiff-legged, I could buy some time. It worked."

I couldn't walk any further. I thought I would die laughing. Becky got downright indignant so I pulled myself together, and we found the car. While I unlocked the door, Becky started swearing.

"Well, what's wrong now?" My effort to stop laughing left me sounding irritated—and I was a little irritated.

"Well, it just fell down to my shoes. I might as well leave it in the parking lot so I won't put it on again." With that, she pulled her foot out of her tennis shoe, peeled off that thigh high, wadded it up, and threw it across the parking lot. It landed in front of the dumpster for everyone to see when daylight came.

She started laughing. "I guess whoever finds that will think some cowboy got lucky with a one-legged woman."

When I finally got control of myself, I started the car. "Well, buckle up and pray we can get back to Frank's Place without being picked up for driving under the influence."

chapter

FOUR

Becky started work the next day so I got up early and went to get coffee at a nearby filling station. When I got back, I found Becky frowning at her cell.

Only one thing made Becky frown at a phone. "How many times has Sonya called?"

"I stopped counting. I think I offended her last night. I know she loves me, but she just wants me to sit around and do nothing. She wants me to get my exercise running from the inevitable. It really drives me berserk."

"I know it does and here I am wishing Mandy paid more attention to me. The grass is always greener you know. Oh, God. Did I really say something so trite?"

"Afraid so. Sometimes you're not very original. Thanks for the coffee. I'll get dressed in a minute and we'll go to breakfast. Where should we go?"

"Let's get brave and go back to the City Café."

"Maybe we ought to wait and do lunch there? Then you can just drop me off at the drugstore."

"That's a good idea. We can look for a diner around here where we could get breakfast. I'll go ask my friend in the office while you're showering."

"Great." She called over her shoulder, "Maybe you can talk him into cooking breakfast for us."

"I wouldn't want to overplay my hand. I'll just ask about a place to go."

I walked down the steps to the lobby and found the manager reading the morning paper. "Hi. I don't think you told me your name. I'm Linda, but you know that from where I signed in."

"My name is Frank. Like it says on the sign 'Frank's Place'."

I felt appropriately stupid. "Frank, could you tell me a place close around where we could get breakfast?"

"There's a diner about a mile down on the left but it's not very clean. The only other places are a long way. City Café doesn't open until 11."

"Oh, dear. We need to get something to eat before then."

"Let me check my kitchen. I might have something that would tide you over, and I know you ladies are on a limited budget. I'll be right back." He went through a door behind the counter to what I assumed were his living quarters.

In a short time, he came back with two bananas, two apples, and two individually wrapped sweet rolls. "This should hold you 'til the Café opens." He put them in a bag and handed them over the counter.

"Frank, you are the nicest person. Thank you so much. We'll go to the grocery today and get some breakfast food. Could we maybe use a coffeepot in our room to make coffee in the mornings?"

"If you'll be real careful about turning it off. Don't want to burn the place down."

"Oh, my friend and I are both people who double check everything before we leave the house. We'll treat this just like our own house. Thanks again." Thank God, he could not see the inside of my house—not a shining example of taking care of things.

Becky was coming out of the bathroom when I walked in, and I held the paper bag of goodies at arm's length in triumph.

"I knew it. You can talk him into anything. Honestly, we are quite the twosome."

"To be honest, I didn't even ask him. He volunteered when he told me there weren't any places we'd want to go for breakfast. He's a nice person. Kind of standoffish, but he's nice. He said we could make coffee in our room every morning if we'd be careful."

"Good. We can go to the grocery this morning for food, and I'll get a coffeemaker at the drugstore."

"I feel kind of bad about paying him so little. But we can't afford the going rate. Maybe we can think of something nice to do for him."

The small table between the old wing chairs provided just enough room to eat our breakfast. When I drew the curtains back, sunlight struggled to come through the dirty windows. "Maybe we can wash the windows for him and not tell him. Wonder how long it would take for him to notice it?" I felt a twinge of guilt for joking at Frank's expense.

Becky stopped mid-bite. "We should do something for him. He gave us a great rate."

"What could we do?"

Becky, the decorator, kicked in. "We could re-do this room a little. It's a mess really."

"You don't like slumming, do you?"

"Not particularly. It wouldn't take much to make this look better— new bedspreads, cushions, curtains. And a good cleaning."

"I'll stop by the Goodwill store and see if they have anything we could use. Do you think he'd be offended?"

"Well if he is, we'll be gone by the time he could do anything about it. I'm not sure I can spend a week in this room like it is." Becky was always that juxtaposition of kindness and insensitivity.

"I'll check around today. Let's get on the road again." I sang our theme song at the top of my voice all the way to the car. Never mind how my voice sounded to Becky. It fit us perfectly. I pretended not to see Becky's shut up or I'll hit you look.

At the market, we found breakfast foods that didn't need refrigeration and coffee packs that would make clean up easy. Checking out, Becky had to use her credit card for the second time.

Back in our room, I put the food on the dresser, and we got ready to go to lunch. As we were leaving, Becky noticed what I was wearing. "Who're you trying to impress?"

"What do you mean?"

"The skirt."

"Well, if I can convince Tubby we aren't looney bin escapees, I might apply for that job?"

"Hey, that would be great. If we both work, we can get enough money to last a while."

We arrived at the Café as Tubby unlocked the door for the lunch crowd. He greeted us with a smile and took us to a booth in the back. As we walked behind him, Becky made waddling motions with her hands. I slapped her on the arm to say stop. She got the point—just as Tubby turned around.

After I sat down, I looked up and gave him my best smile, twinkling eyes and all. "How are you today? We enjoyed our lunch the other day so much we decided to come back."

"Glad to see you ladies again. Sweet tea for both of you?"

"My goodness. You remembered. Yes, that'll be great."

As Tubby walked away, Becky looked at me with dismay. "I think I am going to gag."

"Oh, hush Becky. I need to get this job and being nice is not going to hurt me—or you for that matter."

We ate a hearty lunch and as we paid the bill at the front, I asked Tubby about the help wanted sign. "You still need a waitress?"

"Yeah. One of my girls is out on maternity leave, and the person filling in for her has quit. I need somebody to work for the next two or three weeks."

"Would you consider hiring someone just passing through town? We're going to stay here a while, and I need some extra money to spend while I'm here."

"Ever wait tables before?"

"Sort of. I waited tables at my house when my kids were growing up. Does that count?"

"Well, I guess it's not much different. The pay's not good—minimum wage and tips."

"Oh, that's fine. Would you take a chance on me?"

"If you can start tomorrow and help out for a couple of weeks. You'd need to get here about 10 to help set up and make the tea. Be finished about 2:30."

"Oh, thank you so much. I'll be here at 9:45. You just tell me what you want me to do, and I'll do it."

Walking out the door, Becky made some snide remark about what he might want me to do.

"God, you have the dirtiest mind, Becky. He's just a hardworking man who needs some help." A few steps down the street, I added, "I hope."

I left Becky at the drugstore, reminded her of the coffeemaker, and continued on to the grocery for the Windex and paper towels I forgot earlier. What is wrong with me, I thought. *I'm almost looking forward to cleaning.*

I changed into the slacks and t-shirt I brought for lounging around the room. The cleaning started with our window. Since we were on the second floor, I couldn't do the outside but only one side clean was better than nothing. After cleaning the window, I had enough time to shine everything I could use Windex on. Becky already had the bathroom spotless. Maybe washing the bedspreads later in the week would freshen them up. All I needed to do was get them past Frank's watchful eye.

I stood looking at the chairs. What on earth could I do to make them look better? They had twenty years of grit and grime on them, and there was no way I could get rid of that. Becky was the interior decorator but, in the meantime, maybe a couple of cushions from the Goodwill store would help.

When I finished shining all the Windex-friendly items, I wet a hand towel and dusted even the bottom and sides of the furniture. The filthy cloth told me that had not been done in a while. I worked up a sweat, but the punch of a button woke the air conditioner from hibernation. It spewed dust all over me and everything else. "Son of a bitch," I yelled. I hoped Frank didn't hear me. Back to square one on the furniture and this time, I cleaned the air conditioner filter and vents before starting over.

When I left an hour later, I stopped by the office. "Frank, you gave us such a good price on our room. We'll do our own cleaning and I'll pick up fresh linens every night."

"Oh, you don't have to do that. I'm glad to help you ladies out."

"I appreciate that, but let us at least do this for you. We really would like to."

"Okay, then. I'll leave the sheets and towels and stuff on the counter with your name on them, in case I'm not in here. Thanks."

"Sure thing. I'll see you later."

Walking out, I saw a battered pick-up truck in the parking lot. I could swear the guy who tried to pick me up at the Wild West Saloon was sitting in the driver's seat. Oh, well, I thought. *Maybe he's a friend of Frank's.*

The Goodwill store was on the edge of town, and I looked around for pillows for the chairs. The locals didn't seem to believe in decorator pillows. As I turned to leave, I spotted some chairs about the same size as the ones in our room. What was even better, they appeared to have slipcovers draped over the arms.

I walked over and picked one up. The fabric was rough to the touch—a sturdy cloth my mother used to call duck cloth. They were clean and had wide green and white stripes. Maybe someone recycled an awning. Anyway, I would be more willing to sit on the chairs with a cover on them. I made my way toward one of the workers.

"Are those slipcovers for sale separate from the chairs? "

"No, ma'am. They go together."

"Oh, dear. I'm trying to help a friend who really can't afford to redecorate, and those slipcovers would be perfect for the chairs. Could you possibly make an exception for me and sell them separately?"

"Let me go ask the boss."

He walked to the back of the store and talked to an older man for a minute. I went back over to the chairs and pretended to be measuring. Out of the corner of my eye, I saw the young man coming back toward me.

"Ma'am, he said he'd sell them separately for $25.00."

"Tell him thank you very much." I walked out pleased with myself—bargain hunting in the Goodwill store was not my idea of entertainment, but it paid off.

Back in the room, I wrestled the slipcovers on and they fit almost perfectly. I had to tuck a little extra behind the cushion, but they looked great. Now the only thing left to do was wash the bedspreads.

The curtains were threadbare and I doubted if they would survive a washing machine. Maybe another trip to Goodwill would be in order.

When I picked Becky up at five o'clock, I didn't tell her what I'd done. Her reaction would be interesting.

She walked in the room ahead of me. "What on earth happened here today?"

"What do you mean?" I could do wide-eyed innocence when I needed to.

"It's spotless. And those chairs have new covers." She whirled around. "What did you sweet talk that poor man into now?"

"Nothing. I stopped by Goodwill and got the slipcovers. What do you think?"

" I think you're missing having somebody to take care of. That's what I think."

"Bosh. Really—what do you think? You're the expert on decorating." Becky's outburst held more than a kernel of truth, and I didn't want to think about it.

"It's great. The new slipcovers make the bedspreads look somewhat anemic though. A small-scale plaid bedspread would go well with those chairs or maybe a solid green. Do you really think Frank will be all right with us doing this?"

"I'll take care of Frank. I'll tell him something."

"Maybe I'll say something to him too. He'll like it when we finish." She sat down and took her shoes off. "What are our dinner plans?"

"I'm tired. Let's order a pizza."

"Suits me fine. My feet hurt, and I just want to rest."

I ordered the pizza and got the Sprite from our cooler.

As I dug in my purse for pizza money, I asked, "Do you think we should call the kids again tonight?"

"Let's wait another day or two. I need to be at my best when I talk to Sonya again. I think I offended her sensibilities last night." She peeled off her hose and stretched out on her bed. "Why do you think she's like she is?"

"I think she bugs you about your health because she can't bear to think about you dying."

"Then what on earth will she do when I die?"

"She'll grow up."

"Well, I guess I might as well just kick the bucket then."

"Don't be silly. Just let her practice being without you—like she's having to do while we're on this trip. Now—let me turn that question around. Why do you think Mandy is the way she is? I really pissed her off last night."

"I've never understood her. You've been so good to her and such a help in all her crises. She can't possibly believe that you said she was disgusting. That is so alien to who you are as a mother." She leaned over and rubbed her feet. "I don't know why she is so distant and ungrateful. I just don't know. But I'm glad you're getting some backbone about her."

A knock on the door signaled the arrival of supper. I picked up the money and opened the door. A young pimply faced teenager stood there smiling with our supper in a box.

"Hello ma'am. It's still nice and hot. Would you like me to put it on the table for you?"

"Why that would be nice. And here's your money and a little something extra for you. Thanks a lot."

The pizza safely on the table, he nodded his head and left, closing the door tightly but quietly. So unlike Mandy, I thought, who rarely closed a door she didn't slam.

As he left, I looked beyond him, and there was that pick-up truck again. What the hell was that guy doing hanging around here, I wondered.

I needed to let Becky know about him. "I declare. The people around here are so nice. I think we picked a good place to stop. Except for one thing. You remember that guy at the bar the other night—the one whose lap I sat in? I just saw him in an old pick-up truck outside for the second time today. Wonder what he's doing hanging around here? He gives me the creeps."

"Where is he?" She peeked out the window. "Is that him in that dirty red truck across from our door?"

"Yes. That's him."

"Do you think he's a friend of Frank's?"

"I can't see them being friends. Do you think he's stalking us?"

"I don't know, but I'm putting a chair under the door knob tonight. If he's out there again tomorrow, we're calling the cops." She picked up the nearest chair and scotched it under the doorknob.

She came over to the table and we ate our supper, hoping that would distract us from that niggling worry in our brains.

I noticed she didn't have a napkin under her pizza. "Don't you drop anything on these slipcovers. I'd never find any more."

"Oh, hush. What do you think I am—a slob?"

"Not with your clean hands fetish, I don't. By the way, didn't you forget to wash your hands?"

"Lord, yes. I'll be right back." She scurried into the bathroom.

Maybe Mandy and Sonya wouldn't be the only people whose behavior got modified by this trip. A girl could hope.

chapter

FIVE

The next morning I dressed for work and realized that Becky's hours and mine didn't work together. While we ate our sweet rolls and enjoyed hot coffee, I brought that up. "How are we going to manage your transportation for work today? I won't be finished in time to pick you up."

"Hmm. Maybe I could hitch a ride in that red pick-up truck." I was glad that she could joke about that. I wasn't there yet.

"Yeah. Why don't you do that? Then I can send the local authorities looking for you when you don't show up for work at the drugstore."

"I need to be there at 1, and you won't be finished at the Café until 2:30."

"Do you think you can drive my car?"

"Sure. It's about the same size as my Civic. I'll go slow and be careful."

"Then you drive me to work and after work, I'll just kill some time in the shops around the square until you get off."

"Alright. Let's get going. Wouldn't want to keep Tubby waiting, now, would we?" She threw our trash in the waste can and reached for her sweater.

"On second thought, you just walk to work. It's not but a couple of miles." I gave her a push toward the door.

I insisted that she drive me to work so I could give instructions about my car on the way. We pulled into a parking spot fifteen minutes later and I got out. "You be careful now. If this car gets wrecked, we'll have to go home. Just remember that. And watch out for that red truck."

She thumbed her nose at me when I turned to wave good-bye, but I noticed she looked in all directions and pulled away slowly.

At the café, I knocked on the glass door.

I smiled at Tubby when he opened the door. "Good morning. What do you want me to do first?"

"Make the tea. Most folks drink sweetened tea, but I'll need one thing of unsweetened too. "

I went to the kitchen, found the large pots, and put water on to boil. I stuck my head out the kitchen door and yelled to Tubby, "How many glasses do you make?"

"Oh, about two hundred. Two-thirds sweet and one-third unsweetened."

While the tea was steeping, I went out front and wrapped the silverware in paper napkins and put it on a tray near the cash register. I made sure all the tables were spotless and dry and that the condiments were in order.

By then it was 10:45, and another waitress came in. A brassy blond, sort of plump, and very friendly. Her name was Shirley. She was more well spoken than I expected, based on her appearance. Of course, she might end up thinking the same about me.

At exactly 11, people began to come in. I guess they wanted to get there early while all the food was fresh. The place stayed busy until 1:45, and it was totally empty by two.

"Wow. You have a good business here."

"Lots of loyal customers. Know most of 'em by their first names."

"Well, I enjoyed my first day on the job. People here are so nice, and they all made me feel right at home."

"You did a good job. I'm glad I hired you. Doug, at the drugstore, said your friend gets along with everybody too."

"She enjoyed her first day yesterday. She's friendly, and I'll bet people liked her. What do you do with all your left over food?" I expected him to tell me how to put it away for tomorrow.

"Oh, I just throw it away. The health department you know. And I like my stuff to be fresh anyway."

"Good, lord, what a waste." I thought for a minute. "Is there a senior citizens center around here?"

"Yeah. There's one about four blocks from here. Why?" I could feel his resistance to that question.

"I just wondered if they could use the leftovers. Maybe we could package it up in take- out containers and carry it over there every day."

"I never thought about that. People might be offended." He continued wiping off the counter while we talked. He looked up in a few minutes and asked, "You think they'd use it?"

"Let me tell you, if I was there I'd eat it. It's delicious."

"Do you want to go check at the senior center and come back and tell me?" He almost looked excited.

"I'd love to do that. It won't take me long. I'll have to get the car keys from Becky, and then I'll be on my way. Will you be here for another few minutes?"

"Not usually, but I'll wait for you."

I practically sprinted to the drugstore. Every now and then, I came up with an ingenious idea and this was one of them.

Becky was at the front counter when I hurried in. She reacted with near alarm. "Is something wrong?"

"No. I just had a brainstorm, and Tubby may let me take the leftover food to the local senior center. I need the car keys to go see if they could use it."

Becky smiled. "The social worker never sleeps." After a brief search in her purse, she handed me the car keys.

I managed to parallel park on the side street beside the center. The lady at the desk looked to be about seventy-five.

"Hi. My name is Linda. I'm working for a couple of weeks at the City Café."

"So I heard. Your friend works at the drugstore, doesn't she?"

"Why, yes she does. Have you met her?"

"No. Just heard she was there. What can I do for you?"

"I'm hoping I can do something for you. Tubby, at the City Café, always has food left over and he just throws it away. Is there any way the center could make use of it?"

"I don't know. We feed our seniors lunch, but they're mostly all gone by now."

"Do you think if they knew they could take a free supper home, they'd stay until 2:30? I hate the thought of all that wasted food."

"Let me ask around tomorrow. I'll bet they'd stay and be glad to have the food. Everybody in town likes Tubby's food. Could you come back tomorrow?"

"Sure. In fact, how about me coming back loaded with to-go boxes tomorrow and just see how it goes?"

"Oh, honey that will be wonderful. You're so nice."

"Well, this just makes sense to me. I hope you don't mind a stranger butting in."

"Oh, no. It's a great idea. And I'll post a sign where everyone will see it and know to wait around until after 2:30. If they want to."

"Good, I'll see you tomorrow." As I got to the door, I turned and asked, "Do you think people will be offended by this? It's not like they need charity. It just seems so wasteful to throw perfectly good food away."

"I don't think they will. I'll be sure the sign says it in a way that lets them know it is not meant as charity. How's that?"

"Great. I'm a total stranger, but Tubby will be the one giving all this. I wouldn't want him to lose friends over it."

"Don't worry. People will understand I think. And if they don't, I'll come up with another way to help them understand it's about not wasting. Thanks so much."

I hurried back to give Tubby the good news. As I pulled into the parking spot he had saved for me in front, I looked in the rear view mirror. There was that damn red truck again. This was getting worrisome. I'd have to put a stop to that old geezer somehow. If he thought we were going to have a roll in the hay, he had another thought coming.

When I told Tubby about taking the food the next day, his eyes lit up. "I'll be sure I have enough takeout containers. Can you help me tomorrow?"

"Sure. I'll stay and dish up the food and take it over to the center myself."

"Oh, I'll help you, and so will Shirley. We can all take some of it in our cars. Let's make sure we have enough take-out containers. I'll take all the leftover sweetened tea, too. Everybody around here loves that." There was real excitement building here. I could feel it in the air.

As I picked up my sweater and purse, Tubby handed me a bag with three take-out boxes fully loaded and three large glasses of tea in a cardboard holder.

"You and your friend and Frank enjoy this tonight. Tell Frank I said hello and to treat you right."

"Oh, he's treatin' us really well. I'll tell him you said hi."

I drove up to the drugstore just as Becky came outside. She looked tired but she still had a smile on her face. "What's that in the back seat?"

"Supper for us and Frank. Tubby sent it home with me. He is so excited about taking the leftovers to the senior center."

"Doug loves that idea, too. He's really a nice guy. He wanted to know if he could talk us into staying longer. We must be the most excitement they've had in a while. How sad is that?"

"I don't think it's sad. I think they just like us. We're not very exciting when you get right down to it."

"But excitement is what we're looking for, isn't it?'

"Yeah. But being appreciated is pretty nice too." I decided to wait until we were locked in the room to tell her about the red truck.

"I guess. But don't forget we're out to have some long overdue fun."

We met Frank coming into the office. "Hi. I've got something here for you. Tubby sent it to you, when he gave us our supper. He said tell you hello."

"Tubby's a really nice guy. He's kind of lonely since his wife died, I think."

"That may be about to change."

Frank's eyes opened wide and he nearly gasped.

"Oh, I didn't mean that. He and I decided to box up all the left-over food at the end of the day and take it to the senior center for the folks to take home for supper. He's really excited about that. We start tomorrow. I think he's about to make a lot of friends."

"Now, why didn't anybody think of that sooner? What a good idea. I'll have to stop in tomorrow and tell him so."

"Well, enjoy your supper. Becky and I are in for the night. We're both tired."

"Yeah. When you first go back to working it's really hard."

I hoped Frank wouldn't decide to up our rent. We weren't making that much extra.

Just as we got to the top of the steps, Frank called out. "If you want to heat your supper up, there's a microwave in the office. On the shelf behind my chair."

"Thanks. We may take you up on that. Have a good night, Frank."

After supper, we both crawled into bed, tired from a day of work. I decided more news of the red truck could wait.

chapter

SIX

When the diner closed the next day, we dished up leftovers assembly line style and poured the tea into Styrofoam cups. We finished by 2:30. Shirley, Tubby, and I loaded our backseats and scotched everything so it wouldn't fall over. We all had been able to park in front of the café when we arrived at work. Tubby must have an in with the local police, I mused. That might come in handy if that damn truck kept showing up everywhere.

Our caravan arrived at the senior center ten minutes later and we began unloading the food. Out of nowhere, there were extra hands to help, and we passed food and drinks along a human conveyor belt. I think every senior in the county was there. Inside, a table was set up for the food and iced tea, and Tubby, Shirley and I stood behind it passing out containers along with smiles and small talk. People thanked us profusely. The people and take-out containers came out almost even, and we divided the remaining containers among ourselves.

The lady at the desk followed us to the door. "You're so nice to do this. The people were tickled to death to get that food. They would never take any kind of charity—they don't need to. But knowing this was going to waste was different."

Tubby turned toward me as if I should answer, so I did. "We had as much fun doing this as they did getting the food. It worked out well for everybody. We'll see you tomorrow about the same time."

On the way to our cars, Tubby looked at me and smiled. "Linda, this is the best thing I've ever been a part of. Thank you for suggesting it. People around here have a hard time living on social security, and so many people live alone and just don't cook for themselves."

"I know. Sometimes I don't either. Tubby, you're the one who gave them this. You are the one they will appreciate. And from what I could see, they already do."

Shirley looked as though she might cry. Tubby was positively radiant, if a chubby, middle-aged man can be radiant. I felt better than I'd felt in a long time—even with my aching feet and that distant thought of a red pick-up truck somewhere out there. We all said good-bye and drove away, extremely content with our day.

It was still a while before Becky got off work so I went to the motel, delivered Frank his supper, and put ours in the room. Just for the heck of it, I checked my cell for messages. There were two calls from Mandy. Nothing urgent but I think she was beginning to feel bad about her outburst. "About time," I mumbled. I would call her later. I wanted to think about how to make the most of this time to change things between us. Once I had a plan for that, Becky and I could enjoy our adventure more.

When I picked Becky up, I could hardly wait to tell her about the senior center experience. "The people were lined up waiting, and they were so appreciative. I thought Tubby was going to burst his buttons with pride, and Shirley was all teary eyed. I felt pretty good myself. And I brought supper home for us when we get to the motel."

"I'm thinking you could just settle right in here, Linda. How much longer are we going to be here?"

"We paid for a week, but we both have to work longer than that. I promised Tubby to work for two weeks. Do you want to leave early?"

"How is your money situation?" *Lord, Becky was beginning to be a planner.*

"I made thirty dollars in tips yesterday and forty today. What is minimum wage these days?"

"I think it's $5.25. So if we both work twenty hours this week that should get us about $200.00. And multiply that by two weeks and we'll have enough to finish this trip in style—sort of." She could also do math in her head. Amazing what I didn't know about her.

"Yeah, but they'll take out taxes and all that. Maybe we'll net about two fifty when we include my tips. And I don't have to report my tips— they're all cash. We eat free at night, so we'll keep most of what we make."

"Sounds like enough to get on the road again. Good. I'm getting a little restless. Where are we going next?"

"What's something you've always wanted to do and haven't done?"

After a short pause, Becky knew exactly what she wanted to do. "Let's go to Las Vegas. I've always wanted to play the slot machines and never have."

"Do you know how far that is?" Without waiting for an answer, I kept talking—a bad habit of mine. "I knew I should have bought a map. I don't think we can get that far."

"Does Branson have gambling? That's probably not too far from here."

"I'll check that out. Maybe that's where we'll go next. I know one thing. I want to go back to the Wild West Saloon for some more dancing. And this time don't wear thigh high hose, for God's sake."

I pulled into the parking spot nearest our room and looked all around for that red pick-up. Nowhere in sight. Inside, Becky did her old hand washing routine. I sat down and took my shoes off.

When she came out of the bathroom, I must have looked at her kind of funny.

"What's wrong with you?" she asked, with more than a little irritation in her voice.

"I was just thinking. We left home for an adventure and to have some fun. Be different than we are at home. But I'm right in the middle of taking care of people again. Maybe it *is* time for us to get on the road again."

"No. Let's stay. Everybody's been nice, except that Earl character, and we don't want to stiff Frank or Tubby. Do we?"

"I guess not."

"Anyway. Doug is beginning to warm up to me and I want some time to see where that goes."

"I think I can guess where it will go." I masked that in sarcasm but I knew it was the truth too.

"Hope so. And how are things with Jake? Think that will go in the same direction?"

"Not likely. For a while, at least."

Becky rubbed her back and thought for a minute. "So what day will we leave?"

"I'm not sure. We checked in on Tuesday. If we're staying for two weeks, does that mean thirteen or fourteen nights?"

"I think it means thirteen nights."

She sat down opposite me while I found my checkbook to look at the calendar. "Looks like we'll be leaving on either the eleventh or twelfth." The date 9/11 always jolted me. I looked up at Becky. "What do you remember most about September 11?"

She looked out the window and grew a little solemn. "Mostly just wanting to hug Sonya and Ralph and the kids. They all came over and we just huddled in front of the TV that night. It was awful. What do you remember most?"

I dropped my eyes and twisted my hands together. "I remember wanting to hug Mandy and her kids, but she thought that was silly. She didn't want to come over and I didn't feel free to go there. So I sat by myself in front of the television crying."

After a brief silence, she asked, "Oh, Linda. Why didn't you come to my house?"

"Sometimes it's hard to let other people, even you, know how disconnected Mandy and I really are. I couldn't face the horror of that day and also letting people know my own daughter didn't want to comfort me or let me comfort her."

Becky got up and did something unusual. She gave me a hug.

I cried in spite of myself. It passed quickly, but I knew we needed to get back to the adventure we'd set out to have. We could get maudlin at home—this trip was for fun.

Smiles greeted me everywhere the next day at the Café. Tubby must have told everyone that taking food to the senior center was my idea. The morning flew by and tips were extra generous.

On our second run to the senior center, even more people greeted us, and we barely had enough food. I hoped Tubby would not start cooking extra—I didn't think he could afford that. Nevertheless, the obvious pleasure this endeavor gave him was as big a payoff as seeing the grateful smiles on the faces of the senior citizens.

When we finished the delivery, I decided to visit the Goodwill Store again. I was hoping to find some bedspreads like those Becky had suggested and maybe some curtains. I had enough in tips to pay for them.

A woman volunteer was on duty and she showed me where I might find something. Both of us looked through piles of donated goods and eventually found two bedspreads and some simple white curtains.

"Does the local laundromat have an iron and ironing board? These curtains are a little wrinkled."

"If you have a few minutes, I'll take them in the back and iron them for you."

"Oh, that would be great. I'm just passing through town, and I'm buying them for someone who's done me a favor. I want to hang them right away as a surprise."

"Oh, I didn't realize you had old friends here. You just wait here. Look around and see if there is anything else you want."

People wandered in and out of the store. All of them smiled and said hello, even though I didn't think I'd ever seen them before. Who knows? Between the Saloon, the Café, the drugstore, and the senior center, I might know everybody in town.

I continued to pick up and look at trinkets and house wares that someone no longer needed or wanted. It amazed me that someone would want everything in here, eventually. Even the chipped ceramic mule that said 'Missouri' on it, which I placed back on the table before someone thought I wanted it.

As I started to the car with the freshly ironed curtains, I heard someone call my name. I looked around and saw Jake coming my way. "Say, where are you going now?" he asked.

"I'm just going to Frank's Place until time to pick up Becky at the drugstore. Where are you headed?"

He smiled and smoothed his hair—an old primping technique I never noticed in men before. "I saw you pull in here and waited for you. I thought we might have some dessert and coffee, if you have time."

"That sounds good. I don't think I've had a dessert since I've been here." I walked toward my car to stash the curtains. "Where should we go?"

"There's a coffee shop right off the square, and they have some goodies to go with the coffee. How does that sound?"

"Great. I have a terrible sweet tooth. Can I follow you there?"

"Why don't you just ride with me and then I'll drop you back here in an hour or so?"

"Sounds like a plan. Let me lock the car." I spread the curtains across the back seat and punched the remote lock button. I couldn't believe I was doing this. But it felt good walking alongside him and talking about this and that.

We drove to Eddyville's version of Starbucks. This time of day, there were only a couple of people there. I ordered hazelnut coffee and a brownie. Jake ordered coffee that seemed to match his personality—robust Colombian. His apple pie a la mode probably wouldn't settle on his butt like the brownie would on mine.

Sitting at an old-fashioned ice cream table with the accompanying hard chairs was just right. When my backside got tired, I could suggest leaving and have an excuse. Geeze, why was I already looking for an excuse? He was a sexy guy and a good dancer—what more did I want?

"Tell me about yourself, Linda. All I know is you're a good dancer and you like Bud Light." He suppressed an outright chuckle but not the impish grin.

"Oh, there's not much to tell. I've lived in the same town all my life. My husband died a few years ago, and I have one daughter."

"Did you have a career?"

"Yes, I was a social worker. And I gotta tell you. I don't ever want to listen to another whiney story." I regretted that as soon as it left my mouth. I wanted to hear his story, even if it was whiney.

"I'll remember that. What's your daughter's name?" He leaned back in his chair, settling in for a long conversation, I hoped.

"Her name is Mandy Caruthers. She's divorced and has the two cutest kids on earth. Now, turn about is fair play. Tell me about yourself." I leaned a bit forward and rested my chin on my hand. An old social work trick to show interest.

"Oh, not much to tell. I ran an insurance agency. My wife and I were married for 30 years before she died. No children and not much extended family left either." We lost eye contact as he told me these things. He must be a very private kind of guy, I thought. Not used to talking about himself.

"You must be lonely." God, there I went again saying things that could be misinterpreted. I was not hot to trot—maybe warm to walk, but not hot to trot.

"I was for a time. But this town's great at helping people pick themselves up and 'start all over again' to quote some song. "

"I think that was a Frank Sinatra song. I loved it."

We continued getting acquainted, and when we finished our desserts and coffee, I decided it might be time to move on. This was feeling entirely too comfortable—and a little tingly.

I glanced at my watch. "I'd better get going. I need to take those curtains to Frank's Place and then go pick up Becky in about an hour."

He did not object and stood up to take our trash to the waste can. "Okay. Let's hit the road." On the way to his car, he stopped and turned toward me. "Would you like to do this again? Or maybe have dinner one night?" He must have seen the surprise on my face. "I don't mean to be so forward, but it's easy to talk to you, and I'd like the chance to do that again."

I took a minute to gather my thoughts before I answered. When we got into the car, I said, "I'd like that, too. But my treat next time."

"Oh, Lord. A liberated woman. Who'd have thought I'd find a liberated woman in Eddyville."

"I'll bet there are more liberated women here than you know about. Does that bother you?" That could be a deal breaker.

"Oh, no. I just don't see many around here. My wife was as independent as—what's the old saying? As independent as a hog on ice?" After a pause, he continued, "It was one of the things I loved about her."

We drove in comfortable silence back to the parking lot at the Goodwill Store. As I opened the door to get out, I asked, "When shall we get together again?"

"How about dinner tomorrow? There's a good restaurant about five miles out of town. We could try that."

"It's a date." I looked at him and continued, "That didn't come out quite right."

"Sounds okay to me." This time he didn't try to suppress his smile. "I'll pick you up at Frank's Place at six o'clock."

"I'll be ready." I waved and turned toward my car wondering why on earth I had just agreed to a date with someone I hardly knew. Becky's sense of adventure was rubbing off on me.

At Frank's Place, I hung the curtains on the valance rod at the window. Then I folded the old bedspreads and curtains and put them in the closet. We'd put the new bedspreads on just before we left. I stood in the center of the room and surveyed my handiwork. All finished except for one thing—I had to figure out a way to wash the outside of the windows. For now, I had just enough time to freshen up before going to get Becky.

She came out of the drug store smiling from ear to ear. After our moment last night, I was glad to see that smile.

"Guess what? Doug's going to give me things to make up personal gift bags to take to the senior center. I think you and Tubby started something. I'm bringing all the stuff home tomorrow." She fastened her seat belt and after a minute she continued, "Doug is a super person. And he's single—widowed actually—and seems really interested."

"I'm glad for you. He does sound like a good guy." As an afterthought, I added, "Between the food deliveries and the gift bags, the two of us are becoming what my mother used to call 'do-gooders'. She said it as a criticism, but I think it feels pretty good."

"Me too. But I still want to go to Branson when our time here is finished."

"Absolutely. Otherwise, before you know it we'll be taking care of the whole town and that's not what we left home to do. Want to go back to the Saloon tonight, since we'll be putting together gift bags tomorrow?"

"Yeah. I'm ready to get rowdy again."

chapter

SEVEN

We arrived at the Saloon at seven. This time, I waited just inside the door for my eyes to adjust to the dark. Earl was at the bar so we made our way to a corner table. "I'll go get us a beer. I want to find out a little more about the bartender."

Becky raised her eyebrows and gave me one of those 'really?' looks of hers.

"I just want to find out some more about his college plans, you dope. He's young enough to be my grandchild. But keep your eye on Earl. I don't want him moving anywhere near me."

"I'll watch. And maybe the bartender agrees with the old Tammy Wynette song—older women make good lovers." Thank heavens, Becky did not choose to sing. But now I couldn't get the tune out of my head. I hoped I wouldn't blurt out the lyrics.

I strolled up to the end of the bar farthest from Earl and when the young man walked over, I ordered. "Hi, there. How about two cold Bud Lights?"

"I wondered when you ladies would come back. We're having dance instruction again tonight, and I know Jake will like it that you're here."

"What's your name? I forgot to ask the other night."

"I'm Henry Forrester. Most folks call me Hank."

"Well, Hank, where do you plan to go to college?"

"I'll go to the state college about fifty miles from here. It's cheap, and I can get home if I need to. My parents are getting kind of old." He wiped up the bar as he talked.

"I'll bet they're proud of you. Not all young folks would care whether they could get home."

"Yes, ma'am. They're proud I'm going to college. They help me all they can. After the first of the year, I'll have enough to start school, and then I'll work here again next summer. It may take me a long time, but I'll finish."

"I guess I'd better get back to my friend. By the way, do you know Jake well?"

"Oh, yeah. His family has lived around here for a long time and he's the last of them. Good family and Jake is the best of them all."

"Oh. Thanks for that information. Nice talking to you. I'll see you before we leave."

"Have a good time. Jake will be here in a few minutes. I'll tell him you're here."

"Thanks."

The moment I got back to the table, Becky asked what I had been talking about.

I rolled my eyes before answering, "I was talking to Hank about his college plans. He's going to work his way through college, and I admire that. He wants to go to school close to his parents—that's impressive too. And he said Jake will be here to teach dancing again tonight."

"Good, lord. You have a thing for him."

"Who? Jake or Hank?"

"You tell me." Her wide-eyed inquisitiveness annoyed me sometimes.

"Neither one. What on earth would make you say such a thing? I haven't had a thing for anybody since George died. But a girl can day-dream." Then I decided to fess up. "Jake and I had coffee this afternoon, and he invited me to dinner tomorrow night."

"You're kidding. And I thought I was the adventurous one. You did say yes, I hope."

"Well, he does have a nice ass, let's face it."

"Well, remind me to look tonight. You know me, I wouldn't dream of checking out a man's equipment."

"Yeah. Right."

When the microphone sputtered to life, Jake invited people to line up for dancing. Becky and I made our way out on the floor, ready for another romp.

"Hey, Linda. Want to come and demonstrate steps again?"

I felt myself blushing, so I was glad the lights were dim. *My God, would I never get old enough to stop blushing?*

The music began and dancing started. This time I didn't even have to count in my head. I had the rhythm of the dance and could relax into the pleasure of it. When a break was declared forty minutes later, I was out of breath and sweaty.

"Wow. I think I'd better sit down and have a cool one."

Jake raised his left eyebrow and cocked his head to one side. "Want to go outside and have a cool one?" Since I didn't know exactly how to interpret that, I declined. But I couldn't help thinking, *maybe later*.

I stopped by the bar for two more beers. Hank had them ready before I asked. "Thanks."

Becky had that 'I told you so' look in her eye.

"Here. Have another one on me."

"How is Jake? You two seemed to be having quite a good time."

"Well, you weren't doing so bad yourself."

"That guy I was dancing with is a good dancer. Of course, he wasn't as friendly as Earl was to you last week. I'm jealous."

"Yeah, right." This was as good a time as any to talk about that red pickup truck. "Actually, I've seen Earl following us or parked nearby several more times, but not today. I'm getting a little worried about him."

"Why didn't you tell me? Good God, Linda. Tell me these things. Do you think he really is stalking us?"

"I don't know what he's doing. But if he shows up again, I'm calling the cops."

"Well, if you don't I will. I want some action, but I'll pick my own 'action figures', so to speak." She looked toward where Earl had been at sitting at the bar, and he was gone. "He's not sitting at the bar anymore. Maybe he gave up on us. I hope so."

The night continued with rounds of dancing and rounds of drinks. By ten o'clock, we were ready to go back to our motel.

I walked by the bar to say good night to Hank. "Hey. We're leaving. Too old for these late nights anymore."

"Nothing old about the two of you. Will we see you again before you leave?"

"Maybe."

"Well, good night. Drive carefully."

In the parking lot, we looked all around for Earl. His truck was still there but no sign of him. Once in the car, I locked all the doors. On the way to the motel, I thought about Hank—particularly about his need for college money.

"Get your head out of the clouds and watch where you're going. We've had quite a few beers, and I don't want to extend my stay with a night in the local jail."

The words were not out of her mouth before I saw flashing blue lights behind me. "Shit. The cops are pulling me over right now. Was I weaving or anything?"

"Not really. You ran off the pavement once, but you do that all the time."

I opened my window after I saw his badge and was sure he was a real cop.

"Evenin' ladies. Where are you headed?"

"Back to Frank's Place. You know Frank?"

"Yeah. Everybody knows everybody here."

"Did I do something wrong, officer?"

"Maybe. I saw you pull out of the Saloon, and then you ran off the pavement once. I wanted to be sure you were okay to drive. Would you mind gettin' out and walking a little for me?"

Becky decided it was time to make her presence known. "Deputy, she can't walk a straight line on a good day. Blood pressure medicine does that, you know."

I opened the door, and the deputy helped me out. *Damn. I must look my age.*

"Now, would you just walk along the edge of the road? I'll watch for any traffic."

I walked as straight as I could, and it was none too straight. When I stepped off the pavement and turned my ankle, I barely caught myself before falling.

The officer's face was a battleground between amusement and sternness. Sternness won. "Ma'am, I hate to do this, but I think I'd better drive you ladies to the motel. Normally, I'd just take you to the station, but I know what you and Tubby have been doing at the senior center and I really don't want to do that. Could I have your car keys and take you home? Then I'll get a buddy to bring your car to the motel."

"Oh, I am embarrassed. We had a few beers at the Saloon, and I guess I can't do that anymore and drive."

I got back in the car and told Becky the new plan. She had a hissy fit.

"Just keep your mouth shut, Becky. At least he's not hauling us off to jail. Now get your purse and let's go." I turned on the blinker lights before getting out. We walked behind the car, and I gave the officer my keys.

Settled in the back seat of the cruiser, away we went, looking like questionable characters being taken in for a grilling. What would Mandy and Sonya think of this? It occurred to me that it might not be a good idea to tell them about it.

As we got out of the cruiser at Frank's Place, I turned toward the deputy. "Thanks so much, and I promise I will not drink and drive again."

"I'll hold you to that promise while you're here. Your car will be right out here in about an hour. I'll tell my buddy to put the keys behind a bush at the front door. I'll let Frank know they're there and he'll bring them in early in the morning. Sleep good."

We made our way up the steps, hoping Frank would not hear us. If he did, he didn't come out to say anything, thank God.

In the room, we fell into our beds—part beer and part relief about not being in a holding cell.

Becky got up to go to the bathroom and yelled over her shoulder. "Well, we wanted to get rowdy again. I guess coming home in the back of a patrol car proves we did."

I was still laughing when Becky came back and got in bed. "I hope we don't get run out of town on a rail."

"Not a chance. We're much too charming. Go to sleep."

Just as I was drifting off, the phone rang. Late night phone calls are never good. I pounced on the phone. A gravelly voice greeted me. "Now that the cops have gone, you want to come out and play?"

I eased over to the window and peeked outside. There sat that red pickup and I knew Earl was in it. "Yes, I'll come out to play. But you need to know I play hardball—I will knee you hard in the balls, if you have any. Now get your bony ass out of here before I call the sheriff to come back and arrest you." I slammed the phone down, and Becky bolted for the window.

"God, what is that lunatic up to? I'm scared, Linda. I think we should call the deputy and tell him what's been happening."

"Let's just sit tight and see if he comes back. I heard him peel out of here after I hung up. Maybe I scared him off."

"Well, I'm not going to sleep, and I am getting dressed right now. You'd better, too. At least we can make it hard for him if he comes back."

"Oh, Becky. If I hear anything, I'll call the sheriff, and they'll be here before he could get in the room." After a second to think, I added, "Don't you think?"

"No. I'm not as naïve as you are. You get your clothes on and put that chair under the doorknob again. I'll keep my cell phone handy and you do too. This is going to be a long night."

I did as told, and one of us looked out in the parking lot every ten minutes. Nothing there. When daylight came, we took turns taking a shower and decided to leave early and stop by the sheriff's office to report the goings on.

It felt funny going into the sheriff's office. Somehow, I had managed not to need to do that before. But it was time to ask for help. Earl was beginning to scare me.

The guy at the desk looked up when we came in. I could have sworn he smirked when he saw us. *I'll bet that deputy had told our story all over the office.* I was embarrassed at the thought.

Becky walked right up and started her story. "I want to report a stalker, please."

The deputy turned his attention to Becky at that point. "A stalker? In Eddyville?" He sounded incredulous.

"Yes, a stalker. He drives a red pickup and keeps showing up everywhere we go. And he parked outside our motel room last night and called to ask Linda to 'come out and play'. Don't you think that qualifies for stalking—or worse?"

"What time did this happen?" The young deputy looked down, pen in hand, to begin his official paperwork.

Becky looked back at me. "What time did we get home from the Wild West last night?"

Before I could answer, the deputy answered. "Oh, I think you ladies got home about 10:30 last night." He kept writing on his form with his head down.

"Well, that's beside the point." I responded with a bit of defensiveness. "What we want to know is what are you going to do about Earl?"

"You know who's following you?"

"Yes. I accidentally sat down in his lap the other night, and he's been following us ever since."

"You accidentally sat in his lap?" He looked bewildered, and I knew I'd have to explain that little tid-bit.

"Yes. I can't see when I first go in a dark place and when Becky told me to sit down, I did. Unfortunately, Earl was already sitting there."

Becky whirled around to face me. "So now you're blaming me for this?"

"No. I'm just telling the officer how I came to sit in Earl's lap." I tried to discreetly shush Becky and get a grip on my mouth.

The deputy smiled openly now. "Oh, you ladies don't have to worry about Earl. He's a local, and he's harmless. Just don't make him mad, and he'll eventually go away."

"Well, it's a little late for that advice. I'm pretty sure I pissed him off last night."

"Could you explain a little? How did you..." he paused, "...make him angry?"

"Do I have to tell you that?" Now I was really going to embarrass myself.

"Yes, ma'am. I need to know that."

"Well, okay. He called our room last night and asked me if I wanted to come out to play. I told him I played hardball and that meant I'd kick him in the balls hard, if he had any. Then I suggested that he get his boney ass out of the parking lot."

This time the deputy put his head down on the desk and laughed. At first, I was offended, but then I got tickled too. All of us had a good laugh, which cleared the atmosphere.

The deputy stopped laughing and said, "I'm sorry, ma'am. I don't mean to take this lightly. I just wasn't quite expecting someone your... uh...someone to say that to a stalker."

"You mean someone my age. Well, I'm not your typical senior. So what are you going to do about Earl?"

"I don't really know what we can do. He hasn't done anything yet—except make you mad. And that's not a crime. Let me get the sheriff in here and see what he says."

He picked up the phone and buzzed another office. "Sheriff, could you come out here for a minute? I have two ladies with a problem I don't know how to handle."

In a minute or so, a man in uniform with a beer belly hanging over his belt ambled down the hall. He had a mustache and bushy white hair. He moved too slow for me to imagine him actually chasing a criminal.

He held out his hand, "Hello. My name's Carl Peters. What seems to be the problem here?"

I looked at the deputy in hopes that he would tell the story—with a few edits.

"These ladies think Earl is stalking them. He has been in a lot of places where they are, and last night they saw him parked right outside their motel room door and he called one of them. She kind of told him off, and now they're worried."

"Excuse me, deputy. I was worried before I told him off. He has no business following us around."

The sheriff dropped into the nearest chair while he listened. "Hmm. Not a good thing to make Earl mad."

"So I've been told. Now what can you do to help us?"

He cleaned his nails with his pocketknife while he mulled over my question. "I'm not sure we can do anything. He hasn't hurt you—just ticked you off." He looked up apologetically. "Excuse my language, ladies."

This time the deputy controlled himself.

"That's okay, sheriff. Sometimes we all have to just say it like we feel it." I sat down as I spoke.

Becky got agitated. "So are you telling us that you can't do anything until Earl hurts one of us? Is that all the help available from the law in this town?"

"Yes, ma'am. That's about right. I'm sorry, but I have to obey the law, and that's what the law says."

Becky whirled around and headed for the door with me right on her heels. I turned back and shot my mouth off one more time. "I guess we'll just have to take care of Earl ourselves. But thank you for listening—and deputy, I'm glad I could give you your daily laugh."

Outside we unlocked the car, got in, and immediately locked it again. All the while, we were looking around for a red truck. Of course, there wasn't one. Even Earl wasn't stupid enough to stalk us at the sheriff's office.

"What are we going to do?" I asked. "We need to stay here and make some more money, and I want to get to know Jake better. Actually a lot better."

"Same here about Doug. But I'm scared."

"Let's just go about our business today and talk about this tonight. Just be watchful and don't be by yourself anywhere."

"Okay. But we need to make a plan tonight." She buckled her seat belt and looked over at me. "I'm beginning to understand people packing heat.

After our food delivery that afternoon, I decided to stick around the senior center. I could rest my feet and not have to drive back and forth or be alone. I noticed several people stayed to talk, and I thought it might be nice to get to know some of them.

Walking over to the lady that always seemed to greet people at the front, I introduced myself. "I don't think I've ever really introduced myself. I'm Linda Burton."

"I'm Lydia Walker. I'm glad to meet you officially. You've brought a lot of smiles to this center."

"Really?" I took my sweater off before continuing. "You know, it's Tubby that people need to thank for this. He loves bringing his food here for the people to take home with them. Do you think people would mind if I hung around for a while? I notice that some people stay late."

"Sure, stay with us. Let me introduce you."

We walked over to a long table where folks were sitting. It filled the center of a large rectangular room with metal folding chairs around the walls and plastic chairs at the table. There were several men there and a few women, sipping coffee and chatting among themselves.

"Hey. Linda would like to stay and talk a while. Mack, get her a cup of coffee, would you?"

While Mack went for coffee, Lydia pulled two more chairs up to the table. I was glad she was joining us—I wanted to get to know her.

I looked around the restored cottage. The large room we were in had been divided when it was a home. I could see where they had opened up a wall and left short sidewalls. Probably had been a living room and dining room. "You have a really neat center. Did you folks restore the house?"

A man with white hair and a ready smile answered. "Yeah. Mrs. Brown left the house to the town—didn't have any children—and all of us pitched in to turn it into this senior center. By the way, my name is Harold."

"Glad to meet you, Harold." After looking around a little more, I said, "There must be a lot of talented people around here if you did all this work yourselves."

Another man spoke up but didn't introduce himself. "Well, let's see. Harold is a retired plumber. I'm a retired building contractor. Joe, over there, is an electrician. And there are a lot of other skilled people around here."

Lydia added some names to the list. "I used to be a teacher. That didn't help a lot with the remodeling though." She looked to her right. "Mamie, who helps me out in the front, is the Baptist preacher's wife. She used to make wedding cakes for folks when we had a lot of young people. Great cook. And she plays piano for our sing-alongs too."

I had not seen Mamie before. I turned to her and extended my hand. "Hi. My name is Linda Burton. I'm glad to meet you. I used to be a piano player, too."

"Really. I hope you'll play for us sometime. I'm getting pretty rusty myself."

"Well, my friend Becky, and I aren't going to be around but another couple of weeks at the most."

Harold spoke up. "Don't guess we could talk you two into staying here, could we?"

"No, but we're going to hate to leave. We took off to travel as far as we could on our savings, and we need to get going again." Savings was a bit of a stretch but why admit that, I thought.

The talk continued, and I learned more about these nice people. I had an idea and turned to Lydia to see how she liked it. "You have a lot of active retired people here. Have you ever offered your services to people in the community? Back home, I'm always looking for someone to do things around my house."

"No. We've never considered anything like that." She looked around the table. "Do you all think that's something that would work around here?"

With only a brief pause, heads bobbed up and down, and everybody talked at once. Harold finally held up his hand for quiet. "I like that idea. How many of you wish you had something to do *and* some extra cash?"

All hands went up. Looking around the table, I saw perfectly able-bodied people who needed a way to fill their time and their coffers. This might work. Once a social worker, always a social worker, I thought to myself.

I needed to get going but, being who I am, I spoke up one more time. "Why don't you put together a list of services, decide on an hourly charge, and then post it here and all around town? I'll bet you'd get more business than you could handle."

"Linda, are you sure we can't talk you and your friend into staying in Eddyville?" Mamie's sincerity was obvious.

"I don't think so. But if I ever lived anywhere but home, I think I'd choose this little town. I can't remember enjoying myself this much anywhere else." Or being scared out of my wits by a stalker, I thought.

I got my purse and sweater before going to the large refrigerator to get my three take-out boxes. When I walked past the table, I waved and smiled. "I'll see you guys tomorrow. Take care. Good luck with selling your skills."

It was only 3:30, so I drove out to the antique store where we stopped that first day. The owner was nice, once she got over thinking we were shoplifters, and I wanted to buy something from her before we left.

When I opened the door, the tinkling of a bell let the proprietress know someone had entered. She came out of the back and broke into a smile when she saw me.

"Welcome back. I wondered if I'd see you again before you left."

"I want to find something to take with me as a momento of this place. We've had such a good time getting to know people here."

"The town has had a good time getting to know you and Becky, too. Look around and see what you can find. Is there anything in particular you're interested in?" Apparently, everyone knew our names.

"I like to buy paintings, and I noticed you had quite a few. Are any of them by local artists?"

"A couple. What kind of art do you like?"

"I like what I call character paintings. People whose face shows character—not portraits but character studies."

"I think I have just the thing." She motioned for me to follow her. She was about my age and appeared to be very fit. She moved with a certain grace, and she had more than a hint of a waistline. I should be so lucky, I thought to myself. *Or maybe I should work out more often.*

"Here. Take a look at this." She held up the most striking painting. The woman subject faced the painter, but was looking away from the artist with the most haunting expression. There was a sort of impressionistic forest behind her. Her scarf was blowing to one side. Her eyes were so sad they made me want to weep.

It was a minute before I could say anything. "That is literally breathtaking. I will take it, if you'll hold it 'til we are on the way out of town. I don't really want to store it at the motel. Do you know who painted this?"

"Not really. There's a name in the corner, but I didn't recognize it. It's Bitsy. Just one name."

"Whoever it is is an extraordinary artist. I hope I can find some more work by that person."

As we walked back to the front of the store, I turned toward her. "I don't know your name. I'm Linda Burton."

"My name is Helen. Helen McKenzie."

"Helen, I love your shop, and I absolutely am in love with that painting. I'll pick it up as we're leaving."

"You're going to stay for the ceremony I hope."

"What ceremony?"

"The 9/11 ceremony. Every year we gather on the square for a candlelight ceremony, and we announce our local hero of the year."

"How wonderful! We aren't leaving until the morning of the twelfth. We'll be sure and come. What time will it be?"

"Starts at 7 o'clock."

"Then I'll see you there and again on the way out of town the next day. Thanks so much. I'm glad we had a chance to talk."

Driving out of the parking lot, I realized I had not even asked what the painting cost. Oh, well. I'd use Becky's credit card. I didn't want to go back, get in and out of the car again, and watch who was behind me. This watching over my shoulder was a pain in the neck—literally.

When I parked in front of the drugstore, Becky came out and waved me in. She needed some help bringing the stuff out to the car for the gift bags. We loaded the trunk and the back seat with the help of Doug, the pharmacist.

"Ladies, thanks for doing this. I'm happy to donate the products, but I couldn't put together gift bags. I hope you two decide to stick around."

Becky had a smile that my father would have described as 'a horse eatin'sawbriars' look. "We love doing things like this. You'll be proud when you see how we put it all together, I promise."

"I have no doubt I will be. I may come over to the center tomorrow to help pass them out."

"I assumed you'd be there. I think I'll make stickers for the bags that say 'Thank you for your business.' "

Doug turned and went back inside and we drove off slowly, so as not to disturb the many bags and boxes. We would have our hands full to do this in one night, especially since I couldn't help until after dinner with Jake. I knew Becky—she'd want to make the bags pretty before distributing them. In addition, we'd have to label them men's and women's or the guys would go home with fru-fru lotion and the ladies with heavy-duty razors. Actually, a couple of women I'd seen at the café might make good use of a razor.

We hauled all the stuff from the car into the room and once that was finished, I had to dress for my date. "Jake and I are going to dinner tonight. He's picking me up at six. But I'll help get these bags finished when I get back. We won't be late. I'm already wondering if I should have agreed to this."

"For heaven's sake. Of course you should go. You two are good together. See where it goes. I'll get most of this done before you get back."

"Okay. But I will make an early night of it."

As I gathered things to take into the bathroom, Becky couldn't resist another sassy comment. "Might want to use extra lotion. You don't want rough skin tonight."

"Hmmph. There won't be any skin to skin activity going on."

"You never know. I speak from experience."

"I won't even ask how recent that experience was." I ended the conversation by closing the bathroom door. She might have been kidding, but I was concerned about that skin-to-skin thing. I was not ready for that. I needed to keep this light and impersonal. If that was possible.

At exactly 6 o'clock, there was a knock on the door. I liked that Jake was punctual.

I opened the door, purse in hand, ready to leave. On the way to the car, I asked, "Where are we going?"

"It's called Forsythia Hill. It's a family owned restaurant, and it's been there a long time. I think you will like it."

"I saw that when Becky and I were driving around one day. It looked nice."

Indeed, I did like it. The company was interesting, the food divine, and a glass of wine was a welcome change from Bud Light. My view across the table wasn't bad either. This had to stop!

Waiting for dessert, I reminded Jake we needed to get back early. "I promised to help Becky with some gift bags for the senior center. It was Doug's idea, but he wanted us to put the bags together. "

"I'm glad he asked. He is not exactly creative. But he is a really good friend and a good man."

"I hope so. I think Becky kind of has a thing for him."

"That would be great. His wife died about five years ago and he's lonely. His two children live in California, and they don't get home often."

As Jake paid the waitress, he continued. "Maybe we can do that teenager thing called double dating sometime."

"That would be fun. Becky is a hoot and always livens things up."

" Are you saying I need livening up?"

By this time, I knew that twinkle in his eyes always signaled teasing.

"Well, I plead the fifth."

"I promise I can get a lot livelier, if you'd like." His eyebrows arched into a question mark.

My arched eyebrows had a whole different meaning. "I think it's time to get back and help Becky."

Back at Frank's Place, Jake walked me to the room, and I let myself in. Clearly, I shouldn't have worried about hurrying back. Doug was there, and he and Becky struggled to cover themselves and sit upright on the edge of the bed.

"Should I go out and come back later?" I could hardly contain my mouthful of laughter.

"Give us a few minutes. And use that time to get some control over that mouth of yours."

We stepped back out into the hall. "Well, I guess Doug is not lonely anymore."

Jake laughed outright this time. "Becky either. Does that bother you?"

That was a good question. Was I bothered or jealous? I didn't know. "Becky is a little more spontaneous than me. But that's none of my business. I was just embarrassed to walk in on them."

The door opened, and we went into the room as if nothing had happened. I said goodnight to Jake, and he and Doug left together.

"Well, I'm glad you got some help while I was gone." Sometimes my sarcasm was the best communication tool in my arsenal.

"Oh, yes. That was helpful—really helpful." She couldn't stop smirking.

"I can only imagine."

"You need to work on that imagine thing. Reality is a lot more fun."

I could see the gift bags on the floor under the window. I guess there was more than one kind of help going on. I was glad—I didn't want to be messing with gift bags.

As we got ready for bed, for the first time that night, I brought up the subject of Earl. "What are we going to do about Earl? There is a big 9/11 ceremony I want to go to, but I can't enjoy it if I have to look over my shoulder all night."

"Well, I talked to Doug about it today. He wasn't especially surprised by what was going on, but he was concerned. Have you talked to anyone about it?"

"No. Somehow, it didn't seem right to talk to Tubby. Maybe I can talk to Jake. But what can they do?"

"At least they could watch our backs. And it's a good excuse to talk to them privately."

"Well, getting better acquainted has taken a back seat to safety for me." I was beginning to think I really was a wuss.

"No reason we can't do both." Becky looked over with a grin.

"Okay. Let's just be extra watchful, and I'll try to find Jake tomorrow and talk with him. I didn't see Earl today so maybe the sheriff talked to him."

Unfortunately, we were both sound asleep before the ten o'clock news came on. It was a newscast we needed to hear.

chapter

EIGHT

The next day there was a strange aura at the cafe. Everyone was whispering and looking serious. Yet, when I came close to them, they got quiet. Everyone just hushed. If I didn't already know these people liked me, my feelings would be hurt.

When I was at the counter getting some iced tea, I asked about it. "What's going on, Tubby? Everybody is whispering, but as soon as I come close, they clam up. Is my skirt tucked into my panty hose or something?"

He blushed. "Linda. For heaven's sake. Don't you think we'd tell you that? People around here are just always afraid somebody is eavesdropping on them. Lots of times they are. But today they're talking about the news about Earl."

"What news about Earl?" I hoped the whole town didn't know about our conversation with the deputy and the sheriff.

"They found Earl behind the Wild West Saloon. Looked like he had been dead for a while. Not quite sure what killed him—or who."

My heart was racing, and I could barely stand on my trembling legs. "Do they think he was murdered?"

"Like I said, they're not sure. Waitin' on Doc to do an autopsy. He's also the county coroner."

"When will that get done?"

"Should be finished by tomorrow, I think. Earl was a strange man, but he didn't deserve to die alone behind the saloon. I think folks are feeling kind of guilty about how they treated him."

"Let me know when you know what happened to him. At least people weren't talking about me today." Or so I hoped.

The senior center was buzzing too. But again, for some reason, they didn't want to talk to me. I was beginning to be glad we were leaving soon. I did not like feeling shut out.

As soon as we passed out the last container of food, I got out of there and drove straight to Frank's Place. I stretched out on the bed and the next thing I knew somebody was banging on the door. I looked at the clock and saw that it was six o'clock. *My God, I fell asleep.*

I struggled to my feet and went to let Becky in. At least I hoped it was Becky. Relieved to find her there, even if she was looking pretty ticked off, I went back into the room.

"Where the hell were you? I've been worried to death."

"I'm so sorry, Becky. I laid down and fell asleep. Who brought you home?"

"Doug drove me, and he's waiting downstairs to be sure you're okay. I'll be right back."

She hurried down the steps and was back in a flash. "What's wrong? Are you okay?"

"I'm fine. I must have been overly tired. Did you hear about Earl?"

"Yes. And I'm nervous. You don't think they thought we had anything to do with that, do you?"

"I certainly hope not. I can't decide whether to talk about it or not, but the whole town is talking about it. And it bothers me that they're not talking to us about it."

"I say we just keep our mouths shut—hard as that is—and see what happens."

"Maybe we should just pack our bags and leave tonight."

"No. We don't want to look like we're running. Let's eat supper and then make an early night of it. What did you bring from the diner?"

"Nothing. We ran out of food today for the first time. Want another pizza?"

"Not really. You rest, and I'll go talk to Frank. Be right back."

I stretched out and flipped on the TV. I ran the channels and found a "Golden Girls" re-run. I wondered what they would do if they had a stalker that got murdered.

Becky opened the door and held a bag of goodies at arm's length. "Frank gave me some fruit, cheese, and a Sara Lee cake. Think that will keep you 'til morning?"

"Definitely. I need some down time. I don't know what's come over me."

"Too much excitement, I guess. Between working and watching out for Earl, it's been a hard week or two." Becky not being sassy made me even more worried.

We each put our supper on the nightstand and munched while we watched mindless TV. Before long, we were fast asleep. I woke up during the 10 o'clock news, turned the TV off, and rolled over for more much needed sleep. I woke an hour later to hear someone banging on our door. *Oh God, I hope that is not the sheriff.*

I struggled into my robe and slippers and shook Becky awake. I made sure the chain was on the door before opening it. When I peeked through the crack, my worst nightmare came true. There stood the sheriff, in all his rotund splendor.

"Sheriff, is something wrong?"

"Yes and no. Could I come in for a few minutes?"

I removed the chain and opened the door. Sheriff Carl walked past me. One thing's for sure, I thought, if we made a run for it he'd never be able to catch us.

Becky stood right in front of him and asked, "What is so important that you would wake two senior citizens in the middle of the night?" I recognized fear in her voice, but the sheriff would only hear irritation.

"I thought maybe you ladies would like to know the result of Earl's autopsy."

We both stopped breathing. This was it. We would either be on our way in a few days or spend the rest of our life in prison. All we wanted was an adventure and some fun. This went beyond either of those ideas.

I managed to exhale and ask, "What did it show?"

Becky held onto the back of a chair to steady herself, and I forced myself to take a turn looking the sheriff right in the eye.

"He died from a blow to the head. Can't tell whether he hit something when he fell or if he fell because something hit him. Y'all were at the Saloon the night before we found him. Did you see Earl?"

I took a deep breath and tried not to sound terrified. "Yes. We saw him, but he left before we did."

"Did you see him on your way out?"

"No. And we were watching for him. You know we'd been having trouble with him."

"Yeah, I know. Did anybody see you leave?"

"Not really. Hank knew when we left, but there wasn't anybody in the parking lot when we left. Sheriff, we didn't hit Earl in the head, if that's what you're getting at." I could hear my blood rushing in my ears, and I could hardly stand.

"All I know is you threatened him when you left my office, and now he's dead."

Becky stepped forward. "We didn't threaten him. We just said we'd have to handle him ourselves, since you didn't offer any help. God, we weren't planning to do him in."

The sheriff pushed himself up. "Well, I have to ask questions and find out what happened. You all were mad at him, and then he's found dead. I wouldn't go anywhere if I were you." He started toward the door as he spoke.

"Well, we were planning to leave here on the 12th. Are you saying we have to stay here?"

He turned back to look at us from the doorway. "I'm saying I want to know where you are until we get this settled."

"Can we call you every night and tell you where we are? We're on the last road trip we'll ever take, and we'd like to move on."

"Talk to me tomorrow. I'll get your cell numbers, and we can make some kind of an agreement, I guess. Unless there is some proof that you did this."

He looked back from the hallway. "I'm sorry about all this. You've both been a nice addition to Eddyville, but you were pretty mad when you talked to me about Earl. I need to know if you were involved in this whole thing." He tipped his hat and left.

We both collapsed on the bed. I suspected I was as ashen as Becky was. "My God. How could they think we had anything to do with this? Do you think that's why people didn't want to talk with us today?"

Becky dropped her head in her hands. "I can't believe this is happening. What if we get arrested for this? What will we do?"

"I don't know about you, but I'm calling Mandy for help if that happens. Oh, Lord, I hope it doesn't."

Nobody slept after that little unexpected visit. The next morning, we showered and dressed by six o'clock. Thank God, we had finished with our jobs and didn't have to do anything. I could not possibly have kept my mind focused on a job or a task.

Becky came to life after her first cup of coffee, while I was still struggling through my mental fog. "What are we going to do today? I'm scared to leave this room."

"I'm scared not to leave this room. My head keeps saying make a run for it, and my heart keeps saying stay and clear this up and keep our new friends."

"So what are we going to do today?" she asked again.

"I think we should call Doug and Jake and ask them to come over here. We can tell them everything that's happened and ask their advice. You know these small towns have a good old boy system that pretty much runs everything—even the sheriff's office, usually."

"Good idea. Since I've already talked to Doug about this, you call Jake first and let him set the time for this conversation. Make it clear they're invited for talk and not anything else."

"Well, thank you for that advice, Becky. Whatever would I do without you?"

Jake answered on the second ring. That probably meant I woke him up. "Jake? This is Linda. Could you come over to Frank's Place and talk to me about something?"

From his response, I suspected he knew what I needed to talk about. "Thanks. I'll expect you in about half an hour. I really appreciate it."

I turned to Becky. "Okay you call Doug." In my most sarcastic tone I added, "And be sure he knows you're not inviting him over for sex."

"No problem, you smart-ass. We already did that—remember? So I know he can be real comforting." She smirked and wiggled her eyebrows, before she hit speed dial—much the way she lived life.

Thirty minutes later Jake and Doug appeared at our door together. Doug gave Becky a full body hug, and Jake and I managed something between a Hollywood peck on the cheek and an embrace.

I wanted to get this story told so I rushed right in. "Ya'll know Earl was found dead behind the saloon. You may not know he'd been stalking us, and we reported him to the sheriff. Now the sheriff thinks we killed him. I'm scared to death. We may be mouthy, but neither one of us would hurt a fly."

Jake reached over and held my shaking hand. Every time I put this in words, I couldn't stop shaking.

"Linda, we knew about what was going on. Doug told me after Becky told him. I'm sorry if you didn't want me to know, but Doug and I both wanted to kind of watch out for the two of you. We know you didn't kill Earl. I can't imagine what the sheriff is thinking."

Doug stood and walked over to the window. "Does he have any evidence of any kind?"

"I don't think so. He told Linda and me he wasn't sure if Earl died by hitting his head on something when he fell or falling after someone hit him in the head."

Jake shot out of his seat. "Well, hell. Let's go look for some evidence. That damn fool sheriff should have looked before he came to talk to the two of you. God, he's stupid."

All four of us piled in Doug's car and drove out to the saloon. Earl was found lying near the back of the dumpster. He probably went out there to take a leak and died with his wrinkled, old wiener hanging out, I thought.

"Okay. Everyone look for anything he might have hit his head on. In addition, let's hope it is not moveable. That would prove he fell on it rather than being hit by it."

We moseyed around squinting at everything on the ground, attached or not. We looked like four old people who had lost their vision and their way.

Jake found something first. "Here. Look at this. There's some kind of stain at the corner of the dumpster."

We gathered at the corner and looked, despite the fumes from food, beer, and God knows what else that emanated from the dumpster. Unfortunately, I spotted a ketchup bottle hanging out of the dumpster, and it had dripped onto the outside corner. We resumed our odd little parade around the dumpster. With each circle, we went further out trying to find something too heavy to lift and with a bloodstain on it. In the process of widening the search, I was amazed at what one could find near a dumpster. It was a nursing home for junk. We found beer cans, liquor bottles, food, cigarette butts, and items abandoned once they were no longer useful, including condoms.

Jake raised his hand and stopped us. "We don't need to look too far out. He was found near the dumpster. So if he fell and hit his head, it has to be something close to the dumpster."

Jake was smart. If I didn't wind up in jail for murder, this might work out. "Okay. Let's each take a side of the dumpster and look again. Surely, we missed something. Or someone really did hit him in the head and took the weapon with them."

Becky reacted to that idea. "Good grief. If that happened, the sheriff will never have any evidence. I don't see him searching far and wide for evidence. We're going to end up in prison. I just know it."

Doug decided it was time to take charge. "Becky, take a deep breath and try to think straight. You and Linda left the bar, and the bartender knows about what time you did that. The deputy stopped you on the way home, and he has a record of that. Even if we don't find anything here, we can get those two pieces of information and prove you did not have time to commit murder out behind the dumpster. Now let's look one more time and see if we find anything. And don't forget, he could have fallen and just hit his head on the asphalt. That could do enough damage to kill him. Then we are going to get a statement from Hank and take that to the sheriff's office along with the time the deputy stopped you. I don't know why I didn't think of this before." I could see Becky's body and face relax. Mine was still in a bit of a knot.

We went back and forth along each side of the dumpster, and nobody found anything. A lazy sheriff was not going to see anything that we didn't see.

On the way back to the car, I asked, "Where can we find Hank this time of day?"

Jake took my hand again and gave it a squeeze. "He'll be at his folk's house I imagine. It's not far from here. Doug, do you mind driving by there right now? I'll call Hank and let him know we're coming."

"Not at all. I want this mess cleared up before the ceremony tomorrow night. I want to be able to enjoy that and I won't enjoy it until the sheriff is put in his place."

In a few minutes, Doug turned off the main road and drove down a gravel road toward a white farmhouse with black shutters and a red front door. Even though it needed some work, it was a welcoming place.

We parked beside the driveway and walked up to the door. The steps and the porch were weathered but clearly enjoyed. There were three rockers for sitting and watching the sunset. It appeared that two of those rockers had been used regularly for many years.

Our knock on the door went unheard at first. When Doug knocked a bit louder, we heard footsteps inside. The door opened and a white haired man with a cane greeted us.

"Hello there, Dave. Could we talk to Hank for a minute?" Doug knew everyone in town and especially the older people who had so many prescriptions.

"Sure. Come on in." He opened the door wide and stepped back.

Jake introduced Becky and me. "Oh, I know who these ladies are. Hank has told me all about them. Nice to see you." He bowed his head in greeting and respect. I hoped he didn't know he might be greeting future jailbirds.

Dave called up the steps as we walked by. "Hank. Somebody to see you."

We sat down in an old-fashioned parlor. I had the feeling it had not been used, or cleaned, in a very long time. The furniture was dusty and drapes closed out the sunlight. It wasn't easy growing old at home—it sure as hell wouldn't be easy in prison.

Hank strode in a few minutes later. "Hey, you guys. What's up?"

Doug stood to greet him and explain our predicament. When he finished telling the whole sordid mess, he asked the question we all needed an answer to. "Do you remember what time Linda and Becky left the Saloon?"

"Actually, I do. Linda came by to say good night and when she did, I looked at my watch and commented on them leaving so early. Why?"

I regained my lost spunk and took the conversation from there. "Well, since the sheriff almost accused us of killing Earl, we need to prove that there was not enough time for us to commit murder between leaving the bar and being stopped by the deputy for DUI. We're hoping you can give us that proof."

"Anything I can do to help. That sheriff is nuts. You two didn't do that, even if you were upset with Earl. Good grief. What's gotten into Carl?"

"Thank you, Hank. Your statement is all we'll need I think. That and the time the deputy stopped us. Would you mind following us into town to talk to the sheriff?"

"Not at all. I'll get my jacket and let's be on our way. This is ridiculous. When I finish college, I may run for sheriff."

Our two-vehicle caravan arrived at the sheriff's office at exactly ten o'clock. I had learned the value of noting the time. Jake went in ahead of the rest of us to find out the time the deputy stopped us. Turns out, he had driven the car to the motel, but it was later than when we got stopped. By the time we all gathered in the outer office waiting to see the sheriff, everything was in place to prove our innocence.

The sheriff waddled out and waved us into his office. "Have a seat." He plopped into his oversized chair—with his oversized feeling of power and pea sized brain. "What can I do for you?"

"For openers, you can apologize to these good ladies for accusing them of murder." Jake had worked up a head of steam and I was happy to let him take care of things.

"I didn't accuse them of murder. Just told them I needed to know where they were until we got to the bottom of this."

"Same thing. All you need from them is proof of their whereabouts at the time Earl died. We have that for you. I believe Doc said the time of death was between 11 and 12 the night before he was found. Hank knows Linda and Becky left the Saloon at 10, and your own deputy stopped them at 10:10 to be sure they were okay to drive. He took them to Frank's Place and had me pick up their car and take it there later. So they were at Frank's Place about 10:20, with no vehicle to drive anywhere. Is that proof enough for you?"

The sheriff looked at Hank. "You willing to swear to that?"

"I am."

Jake continued, "And we have a copy of the warning your own deputy gave Linda. The time is 10:10." Jake handed a piece of paper over the desk. Sheriff Carl looked at it, pretending he didn't know exactly where to find the time of the warning. "And I'll give a sworn statement about what time I drove their car to Frank's Place. I guess all of this gives them an airtight alibi."

The sheriff looked at Jake. "I'll keep this, and you and Hank will need to make those sworn statements to the deputy."

"And you still need to apologize to Linda and Becky." Jake wasn't giving up.

"Ladies, sorry I scared you." The jackass didn't even look at us when he spoke.

Before I could say anything, Jake lit into him again, jabbing the air with his index finger. "That is not what you need to apologize for. You need to apologize for even thinking they might have killed someone. Now apologize for that." He slammed his fist on the desk, and the sheriff flinched.

With a sweep of his stubby hand and a fake bow in my direction, he sputtered, "I am sorry I even had such a thought." He turned a sarcastic look toward Jake. "Now can I get on with my day?" Jake whirled around and left the office with the rest of us right behind him.

In the hallway, I collapsed onto Jake's shoulder, and Becky hugged Doug until his eyes bugged out. As Hank walked down the hall to give that sworn statement to the deputy, he turned around and called to us. "When I go to college, I'm studying criminology and coming back here and run for sheriff. I think we need a new one."

We all raised our arms and cheered him on, as if he were a star quarterback making the winning touchdown.

After Jake finished his statement to the deputy, he and Doug drove us back to the motel. Jake gave me a hug and explained, "Sorry to just leave, but Doug has to get back to the drugstore, and there are a couple of things I have to do before tomorrow's ceremony. Can we get together later, maybe?"

"For sure. And how can I possibly thank you for what you've done?"

He smiled, and said, "I'll think of something." This time he gave me a real kiss, and I liked that a lot more than that peck on the cheek earlier in the day.

In our room, Becky and I just sat in a heap at first. I made a pot of coffee, and as I handed her a cup, Becky sat up in her chair and looked at me. "I don't think I have ever been so scared in my life. Thank God for Doug and Jake."

"Amen to that. I guess there is no more doubt about our relationship with the two of them. I don't know about you, but it feels so comfortable for me. It's nice to have someone to lean on, and I've never been much of a leaner. Course, I've never been accused of murder before either."

"Yeah. I kind of like the leaning thing too. What do you want to do today?"

"I say we just hang out here. I'm tired, and Jake's busy all day. Do you mind?"

"Not at all. We'll put on our pajamas, watch TV, and order pizza for lunch. I'm pooped."

"Maybe the guys will call later and we can go to dinner with them. Or not. I could use some extra sleep."

Becky turned to look at me. "Are you alright?"

"I'm fine. Just tired. It's been a shitty day."

chapter

NINE

On the morning of 9/11, I finished my waking-up routine and asked, "What are we going to do with our last day?"

"I need to just sit still for a while. We should get to the square about six o'clock I think. That means we have time for a late lunch and then whatever we want. Any ideas?"

"Let's rest a while and then eat lunch at the City Café and go pick up my painting. After that, all we will have to do is pack and get dressed for tonight. I can't wait to see who their hero of the year is. Wish I could nominate Doug and Jake."

"Who do you think it will be?"

"I have no idea. Wonder who the past winners are."

We sat quietly for a while, drinking our coffee. In a few minutes, Becky went to the bathroom, and I began to pack the things I knew we wouldn't need after today. By the time Becky came back into the room, I was almost finished and getting hungry. "Let's go to lunch and then buy some kind of dessert to share with Frank. We need to show him what we did to our room."

"Yes. I'd totally forgotten about that. And my appetite has returned in spades. Let's get going."

I picked up my keys and followed her out the door. As we went through the lobby, I saw Frank and called to him, "We'll be back after while, and we have a surprise for you when we get back. Gonna be here a couple of hours from now?"

"Yep. I'll be sittin' right here. Have a good lunch."

During lunch, Becky looked across at me. "This has been a great three weeks. I'd never have thought I would enjoy such a small place, but I have. Do you think we can stop by here on our way home?"

"Even if I've been scared to death over this Earl thing, I was hoping you'd want to do that. I feel like I have friends here. I think it's going to be hard to say good-bye—especially to Jake. But we'll be on the road again tomorrow."

"Do you want to say good-bye to the guys and show Frank the room and leave today?"

"I think we'd kick ourselves for not staying for their 9/11 ceremony. Nobody does those things better than the good people in small town America." I was looking forward to that, but I also thought saying good-bye to Jake might better be done in the dark.

"You're right. The road can wait one more day. "

"Let's get my painting and then find a bakery to get some dessert for Frank. We'll just invite him up for dessert and surprise him with the decorating." I paused and opened the car door. Then I turned to Becky and asked, "What if he thinks we're inviting him up to look at our etchings?"

Becky laughed aloud. "Frank? I'll bet he hasn't had a thought like that in twenty years."

The antique shop was about two miles from the square. There were no cars around when we got there, and Helen came out from the back as we walked in.

"Hello there. Are you here for your painting?"

"Yes. I thought we'd get it today and then leave early in the morning. I really appreciate you keeping it for me. I didn't ask how much it was."

Helen hesitated. "It's only a thousand dollars."

"Oh, my. I can't afford that. And I don't have a way to get money from home."

Helen burst out laughing. "I was only kidding. It's only seventy-five dollars." She started to the back to package the painting for me.

I poked Becky in the ribs and whispered. "Give me your credit card. I don't have any money with me."

"Well, I hope you have some at the motel," she hissed.

Helen came out with the painting well padded for the trip. "I hope you enjoy this. And I hope you remember Eddyville every time you look at it."

"I know I'll enjoy it and it will remind us of our time here. Thanks again."

Becky held the door open and, once outside, we turned and waved good-bye. Before we got in the car, Helen came running out.

"You all will be at the ceremony tonight won't you?"

"Oh, yes. We're planning to come. See you there."

As we drove onto the town square, I wondered aloud. "There is a bakery on the square and I hope it's open. Let's check it out. We could get a lot of cookies and give Frank some to take home with him, and we could take some with us tomorrow."

"Good idea. I haven't been in the bakery. Have you?"

"No. We've been just about everywhere else so we might as well meet someone new today."

There was a lot of activity outside of the shops, where owners prepared windows for the 9/11 ceremony and hung flags outside each door. The bell on the bakery door jingled as we entered. Smells of butter, chocolate, lemon, and spices gave it a homey atmosphere. A young couple greeted us from behind the counter with big smiles. Powdered sugar smudged their faces, and the young woman had a streak in her hair.

"Good morning. We're Joan and Mike Baldwin. How nice to see the two of you. I've heard the whole town talking about you."

My eyebrows popped up. "Good things, I hope."

"Oh, yes. All about your work at the senior center. We also heard a little about what good dancers you are." They worked at keeping their expressions under control.

Becky was hooked with that last statement. "Our dancing ability? Where on earth would you have heard about that?"

"Hank's a friend of ours. He told us about how much fun you all had at the Wild West Saloon. He really enjoyed watching you."

"He's a nice young man. Working hard to go to college. I hope he doesn't have to work too hard."

Mike spoke for the first time. "I'm sure you know the town is trying to get together some scholarship money for anyone who will come back after college and go into business here. I think Hank might be one who would do that."

"That's great. I hope he gets that. Then he can finish a lot quicker and I suspect he'll want to live here."

"Yeah. He's really devoted to his parents, and he's lived here his whole life."

Becky had been looking at all their baked goods while I was talking.

"What have you decided on?" I asked.

"How about half a dozen of everything?"

The young couple laughed, but I was not so sure she was joking.

"How about a dozen of three things?" I countered.

Mike got a box for our three dozen somethings. The kitchen aromas made me think of home, grandkids, and cookie making. I tried to shake that thought right out of my head. We'd be back there soon enough.

Mike and Becky were into the selection process, and I used the time to talk to Joan. "Have you always lived here?"

"No, ma'am. Mike and I moved here a few years ago from St. Louis."

"How interesting. What made you choose Eddyville?"

"We wanted a small town in need of a bakery and not too far from a larger city. This is close to Columbia, so it met all the requirements. And this building was for sale at the time. So here we are."

"Have you been glad you made the change?"

"Oh, yes. The people here are so nice, and they just took us right in. Local workers helped us renovate this place, and we were up and running in less than six months. Never have regretted it a moment."

Her face reflected the contentment in her words. It was clear she adored Mike and loved what they were doing.

"I think if I ever moved away from my home, this would be a wonderful place to live. However, we're leaving tomorrow. Going to continue our little adventure."

"Well, I am so glad you came in today. I've wanted to meet you. And maybe one day you'll move here, who knows."

"Yeah. Maybe."

Becky was loaded with cookies and ready to move on. We said good-bye and went out to the sound of the bell and the sweet smells of contentment.

Back at the motel, we got ready for Frank's surprise. Feeling more like my old self, I took charge. "Okay. Let's get this room in shape. You clean the bathroom, and I'll make the beds and put on the new bed-spreads. I'm going to pull the curtains across the window 'cause I never figured out a way to wash the outside of the windows."

"Aye, aye, Captain." With a fake salute, she retired to the bath-room with her cleaning supplies. I set about making the room look the best it could. I put the cookies on a paper plate and sat them on the small table where we had been eating breakfast each morning. I even folded some napkins into triangles and lined them up.

Becky came out of the bathroom, wiping her hands. "Let's leave the bathroom door open. He'll need to see how clean it is and see the plug-in deodorizer and candle I put in there. And that little picture of an angel floating on a soap bubble is cute too."

At just that moment, Frank knocked on the door. When he came inside, he looked around kind of befuddled. "There's something differ-ent here. What did you ladies do?"

Just like a man—couldn't figure out what was different. "We de-cided to do a little redecorating to say thank you for the good rate you gave us and all the times you've helped us. We wanted to surprise you." I reached over and patted Frank on the shoulder.

"I hope you didn't spend a lot of money doing this. I was happy to give you a good price on this room. No need for all this."

"We wanted to do something to thank you. Of course, when we come back through we'll expect to get this room." Becky loved to bargain, even when we were doing someone a favor.

"No. I'll put you in another room, and you can fix it up too."

My God, he had a sense of humor. Who'd have thought?

Becky was equally surprised. "Frank, we'll decorate the whole place one room at a time."

"Well, thanks for all this work. It looks better."

I breathed a sigh of relief. "We bought some cookies for dessert. That little bakery on the square is good."

"It sure is. I don't buy much there because it costs so much, but I like it. And Joan and Mike are a real good addition to Eddyville." Frank looked anxious to start on the cookies.

The three of us sat at the little table, and it was a tad awkward. Frank was kind, but he wasn't very social, and I don't think he was used to having dessert with two women.

When we finished several cookies and a cup of coffee, Frank got up and began clearing the table.

"No, no. You're our guest. Sit down. We'll clean up—it's easy. We just throw it in the trash can." I motioned him toward the chair again.

"Okay. But I'm going to have to go help get ready for tonight. Thanks for the cookies. I really like what you did to the room. What room do you want next time?" I saw Frank smile.

I laughed. "I think we'll take this one, Frank."

Becky held out a plate of cookies. "Here. Take some cookies with you for later. You'll work up an appetite decorating for tonight. We figured we need to be there about six to get a good spot for the ceremony. What do you think, Frank?"

"Six sounds about right. Everybody in the county comes in for this, and it's usually crowded." Once he was gone, we indulged ourselves with even more cookies.

"Are you all packed to leave early tomorrow?" I asked.

"What's your hurry? Didn't you just tell me how much you enjoyed being here?"

"I do. Too much. It's going to be hard to say good-bye, and I hate good-byes."

"Well, we are not leaving early. Everybody expects to see us tonight and say good-bye. And I have no intention of leaving without a proper good-bye to Doug."

"Hmm. I wonder how proper it will be."

chapter

TEN

Approaching the square, we could see that parking was not allowed. Yellow tape blocked off the roundabout and cones blocked each entrance. Apparently, Frank was right—everybody in the county must come in for this occasion. We parked three blocks away. Walking back toward the square, it was amazing how many people stopped and talked to us. We knew lots of faces and some of the names, but they all seemed to know us.

We turned onto the square, and it was quite a sight. Each shop had an American flag flying beside the door, and the lighted windows displayed the best of their wares. A small platform stood on the far side of the roundabout, and I could see Tubby, Lydia, Helen, and Jake setting things up. There were luminaries placed every few feet at the edge of the sidewalk. If it stirred the emotions of relative strangers, I can only imagine how the locals must have felt.

I was feeling sentimental about this little town. "Let's walk around the square once more. We'll be leaving early tomorrow and won't be back for a while."

Becky stopped to talk to Mike and Joan in front of the bakery. I wandered on down to the City Café. Tubby had the lights on and the biggest of all the American flags outside the door. I couldn't help remembering the terrible laughing attack Becky and I had when he introduced himself.

I continued walking, stopping to look in windows and talk to people. Hank waved from a distance and came over to talk, as I looked in the hardware store window.

"Hey. I'm happy to see you here tonight. After what the sheriff did, I wasn't sure you'd be here. We're going to miss you girls at the Saloon. Haven't seen anybody else having that much fun."

"Well, we won't judge the whole town by the sheriff. We've enjoyed our weeks here except for that unpleasantness. However, that's behind us, and we wanted to see your special ceremony. Has the sheriff decided what happened to Earl?"

"No, ma'am. I don't know if he'll ever figure it out. We really do need a new sheriff, and I plan to try to be the one to beat Carl in the next election."

I saw Becky motioning for me to come over where she was. She had staked out a spot close to the speaker's platform. "I have to go over with Becky. You want to come too? We're just staking out a good place to watch the ceremony."

"Sure. My parents didn't feel like coming, so I'll just be your 'child' tonight."

"Now, that would make me proud. If I had a son, I'd want him to be like you." We made our way to the other side of the square and squeezed through the crowd to the front where Becky stood. I'm sure people watched and thought how pushy I was. Actually, they were correct. And worse yet, I was somewhat proud of it.

The microphones squawked the way they do when they're first turned on and people began to get quiet. On the opposite side of the square, I could see the police officers and sheriff's deputies lined up, and it looked like the volunteer firemen behind them. I was glad to see that the sheriff was not with them. The deputies and officers all stood at attention, each carrying a large flag. When the sound system sputtered to life and a John Phillip Sousa March came over the airwaves, the officers and firemen marched into and around the square. I must say it was another stirring sight. Knowing so many of these good people made it even better. As I looked around, everyone was looking straight at the procession of flags and standing very straight. The parade stopped right in front of the platform, and the officers and firemen turned in unison to face the people. The crowd became silent in the few seconds before Tubby took the microphone and led the people in the pledge to the flag.

"I pledge allegiance…" It was one strong voice of simple patriotism, and we all held our hands over our hearts. I hadn't done that since grade school, yet it felt totally right here and now. I envied their uncomplicated patriotism and spent just a second wishing I had the same. Even patriotism was complex for me.

The officers, including the deputy who chose not to give me a DUI citation, placed the flags in front of the platform and turned to face the master of ceremonies. Tubby picked up the microphone again. All eyes were on him.

"I thank you all for coming tonight. Brother Johnson from the Methodist Church will lead us in a word of prayer. Brother Johnson."

A stately gray haired gentleman stepped up to take the microphone from Tubby.

"Will you all please bow your heads?"

"Father, we thank you for another year safe from harm. May you guide us in the ways that will keep us all safe. We remember before you those who died on 9/11. We pray for their families, and we pray for those heroes who saved so many lives and helped us feel just a little safer in such a scary time. Thank you God for the good people of Eddyville and our firemen and policemen and all the other people that are true heroes right here in our midst. In Jesus name, we pray. Amen."

The crowd shuffled as they raised their heads and moved around a bit. They didn't talk—just relaxed their stance. Tubby was at the mic again.

"Thank you, Brother Johnson. As you all know, every year we meet on September 11 to remember and to be grateful for what we have. We also select a hero of the year. This has to be somebody who has gone above and beyond to help others. It has to be someone who acts in the spirit of the people of our country in those awful weeks in 2001. The first year we honored our own firemen, some of whom went to New York to help out. The next year we honored Doctor Holloway for treating people whether they have insurance or not. Last year, we honored Mrs. Brown who left her house to the city, and it is now our fine senior citizen center. This year we are honoring two people."

I could hear people whispering and talking among themselves. They clearly didn't know who had been picked for this honor. I tried to think about all the people I'd met, and I couldn't think of anyone who might share this award. Maybe Mike and Joan were the ones. That would be nice. They were so happy and had chosen this as their home—a little different from being born here and staying. But not heroic. I couldn't think of another twosome.

There was some static coming from the speaker's platform, and someone came and adjusted the microphone. Tubby continued. "Many of you know the heroes for this year, but some of you don't. Let me tell you some things they have done." I couldn't believe how confident Tubby was in front of all these people. He was like a different person.

"This year's heroes have started several new programs at the senior center. A plan for using food that usually gets thrown away. A list of services available to the community through the senior center members. They have gotten the ball rolling on a local college scholarship fund. They have become a really important part of life in Eddyville, if only for a short time."

Becky and I looked at each other with jaws dropping.

"These two people simply stopped in Eddyville on their way somewhere else. They have done so many good things for us we decided to name Becky James and Linda Burton as our heroes of the year. Ladies will you come up and accept your award?"

For the second time since I landed in this town, I had tears to deal with. I don't cry, but there I was wiping my eyes and holding Becky's hand as we walked up the four steps to where Tubby stood. He handed us a plaque that read "Heroes of the Year" with both our names on it and the date.

I couldn't speak. Becky, of course, had no problem talking.

"Thank you, kind people. I am sure there are people who deserve this more, but nobody could possibly appreciate it more. We were just going to stop for a day or two, but we have enjoyed three weeks here. It has been a joy to get to know you and your town. We will be back for sure."

By this time, I had pulled myself together, and I reached for the microphone. "You have no idea how much this means to us. We have loved being here and feeling so at home. And to have you appreciate what we did enough to give us this honor is just astonishing. Thank you from the bottom of my heart."

Applause started with Jake, Helen, Joan, and Mike. Hank and others joined in, and I suspected that Doug added that shrill whistle I could never learn to do. Tubby and Frank were smiling from ear to ear. Lydia, Mamie and the rest of the senior center crowd joined them, and soon the whole square filled with the most wonderful noise I ever heard. I closed my eyes and absorbed the moment, so I could relish it when I remembered. Becky was doing the same when I looked at her. When I handed the mic back to Tubby, I hugged his neck, and the applause started all over again.

Tubby turned the speaker back on and quieted the crowd. "Before Reverend Miller offers a benediction, I just wanted to let you know there will be a community memorial service for Earl tomorrow at two. I hope you can be there. He was part of us for a long time and we want to say a proper good-bye." He paused for a second. "Now, Reverend Miller from the First Presbyterian church will offer our benediction."

Reverend Miller faced the crowd. He raised his arm and began. "The Lord bless you and keep you. The Lord make His face to shine upon you and be gracious to you. The Lord lift up his countenance upon you, and give you peace. In the name of the Father, and of the Son, and of the Holy Ghost. Amen."

The ceremony ended, and people began to move about and talk to their neighbors. Lydia walked toward us and gave us both a hug. She leaned over and whispered to me,　"We have supper all ready at the center. As soon as you can get away, come on over."

"How nice. I can hardly wait to sit down and talk with our friends. Thank you for your part in all this—I have a feeling you had a part in it."

She smiled sweetly and walked away.

Jake came up behind me, spun me around, and gave me a hug. "Congratulations! We are all so glad you and Becky stopped in this place. You *are* coming back aren't you?"

"Definitely. We're going to stop on the way back home, and I suspect we will be coming to visit every year. Right around this time. And I'm hoping to see you and Doug in Millersville in-between our visits here."

"Good. I can hardly wait to see you again. Oh—the scholarship fund is coming along. All the merchants in town are contributing and a lot of individuals. We'll have enough soon to announce that it is available for anyone who will come back and live here. I'm pretty sure Hank will be the only one to apply, and I think he meant what he said the other day."

"He definitely meant it. I just talked to him tonight. Oh, I hope he gets it. He's just the nicest young man."

"I'll see you over at the center. Gotta' help clean up now."

I gave him a hug and held on a little longer than I meant to. He gave me an extra, quick squeeze and went toward the back of the platform.

It took Becky and me a while to get around the square and over to the center. We stopped to accept the congratulations of lots of people. I hadn't felt this kind of appreciation in a very long time. I wasn't entirely sure all of Becky's excitement was about the award. She and Doug had been deep in conversation the first few minutes after the ceremony ended. Probably planning a rendezvous somewhere.

We went in the front door at the senior center and were taken aback. Food covered a table on the left. Straight ahead there was a long table all set up for the regulars and some extra people. Someone had put together a red, white, and blue centerpiece of metallic stars, fake sparklers, and what looked like red and blue noisemakers. Streamers went out on each side of the centerpiece almost to the end of the table. There was a banner behind the table that read "Congratulations Becky and Linda".

Lydia greeted us and invited us to start the line down the table buckling with food. There was barbeque, potato salad, slaw, squash casserole, baked beans, and probably ten other dishes. Mamie was serving iced tea at the end of the table. We loaded up and went to sit down.

"No, no. The two of you sit at each end—the places of honor." Harold held my chair and then hurried around to do the same for Becky. Doug quickly found a seat next to her. Others sat down with plates piled high. Toward the end of the line, I saw Tubby, Helen, Jake, and Frank. They must have been the last to leave the clean-up detail.

"Folks, I never had such an honor or so much fun packed into a few weeks. Somebody must have cooked all day to make this feast. Do we get this every time we come through?" I had to get back to joking around to keep from crying.

Mamie sat down near me. "No. Next time you have to cook for us."

"That's a deal. When we stop through on the way home, we'll cook for all of you. It probably won't be this good, but I promise it won't make you sick."

The camaraderie among the people there was comfortable and real. Nothing obligatory—just people enjoying people. We talked and ate and laughed and did it all again. As the regulator clock ticked toward nine o'clock, Mamie quietly left the table. In a minute, she returned with the biggest one layer cake I think I ever saw. She put it on a small table to our right. Everybody got up to look at it.

Becky and I arrived at the cake table about the same time. The cake was huge, with a little chocolate peeking out from under the white frosting. In beautiful blue frosting script, it said, "You came, you saw, you conquered—our hearts."

I couldn't cry again—I just couldn't. I covered my mouth with my hand momentarily and got myself under control. When I put my hand down, my face lit up with pure pleasure. I bent over the table to hug Mamie and since Becky did the same at precisely the same moment, we clacked heads. The almost crying moment gave way to a belly laugh.

"Good thing we are equally hard headed." Becky rubbed her head as if she had been wounded.

"I am not so wounded that I can't ask for the first corner piece with all the frosting. Mamie, I have not had real white frosting since—I don't remember when. Is it that kind with sugar, water, Karo syrup, and egg whites?"

"Sure is. Only kind I ever make."

"I bow to your greater skill. I never, ever had a batch of that turn out right. When we come back, we'll cook except for the dessert. You have to promise to make this exact same cake again."

"I'll be happy to." Mamie's eyes were sparkling in a way I hadn't seen before, as she handed me that corner piece I asked for.

Becky, of course, couldn't miss the opening I gave her. "And all of you will thank Mamie for making sure you don't have to eat Linda's desserts!"

After coffee and cake, people began clearing the table and cleaning up. Becky and I jumped right in to help.

"Now, ladies. You are the honored guests. You are not going to clean up."

"Why, of course, we'll help. You just gave us a huge feast and a wonderful award. We want to help."

"You've already helped this place more than you know. Now you go home and get some rest before you take off tomorrow. And get some leftovers to take with you tomorrow." Lydia was adamant about this.

Good-byes and hugs took a few minutes, before we went out the front door loaded down with good home cooking to take with us. Jake and Doug walked out with us. They both were campaigning for us to stay another week.

"If we stay, you all will have to help us eat all this food tomorrow." I wanted to stay, but a little insistence would feel nice.

Doug brightened at the thought. "That's not a problem. The four of us could polish off this food in short order. If we agree to help with that, will you stay for another week?" He looked at Becky as he spoke.

She and I exchanged glances before I answered. "I think that would be nice. We've been rushing around working, crime solving, and planning to leave tomorrow, but another week would give us some relaxing time."

Jake turned me around to face him. "And it would give us some time to get better acquainted. I'd like that." His look was disarmingly sincere.

"Me too." I turned around and included the others. "We'll see you guys around lunch time tomorrow."

When we were safely inside the car, I burst into tears. For once, Becky didn't say anything, except to ask if I wanted her to drive. I blew my nose and started the car. "Of course not. I don't know what has come over me. I've cried three times this week. Geeze."

"You'll be fine. You thought you were going to have to say good-bye and you never were worth a damn at good-byes. Aren't you glad we're staying?"

"Very." We were uncharacteristically quiet for a few minutes, and then I blurted out, "The next good-bye will be even worse. I'm so bad at good-byes; I don't even go to funerals. I guess you'll have to pay people to come to my funeral when I die."

"Don't worry, honey. I'll throw such a bash when you die, they'll come from miles around for the free booze.

"Smart-ass."

We were ready for bed by ten and more tired than we realized. In ten minutes, the only sound in the room was Becky's soft snoring. Another reason we used to get two rooms. I couldn't stop thinking and get to sleep. It had been such a special night for me. Unappreciated at home, this event seemed to fill a void in me. And thinking of a week with Jake sent tingles to places I hardly remembered. I finally drifted off about midnight.

chapter

ELEVEN

During the following week, all our time was spent with Doug and Jake. We went out to eat, to movies, driving in the countryside, and spent time alone in their homes. Sometimes the four of us went out together, but more often, we spent our time privately. I was pretty sure Becky's time at Doug's house was very different from my time with Jake. I had to get used to these new feelings that I never expected to have again. It might have been easier to just have a one-night stand, but that wasn't what I wanted. I was not exactly sure what I wanted, but I knew that was not it. So Jake and I enjoyed each other's company and some 'almost, not quite' behavior. He didn't pressure me, but I did seem to live with a constant smile on my face.

The night before we were to leave, I woke at two in the morning. Of all things, I was thinking about the one thing we had not done to improve this room. I had to think of a way to clean the outside of the window. I walked over and moved the curtains back. It was country dark outside—no light except from a half moon. There was enough light from our night light to see that the windowsill was pretty wide. I opened the window and ran my hand across it to check for nails. Old and splintered but no nails. I could put a towel over it to protect by backside.

Becky was going to kill me for this, but I finally figured out how to do that one last thing. I shook her by the shoulder. "Wake up, Becky. Wake up."

She jumped to a sitting position. "What's wrong?" She glanced at the clock. "Why are you waking me up at this ungodly hour?"

"I just figured out how to wash the outside of the window. Then the room will be perfect. Get up."

"Hell. If you figured it out, you do it. I'm going back to sleep."

"Get up, you old goat. You have to hang onto my legs to be sure I don't fall out the window."

"Good God, Linda. What are you going to do?"

"I'm going to open the window and sit on the windowsill and somehow manage to get my top half outside and then I'll clean the window. But you've got to stay in here and hold onto my legs so I won't fall out. Now—do we have any paper towels?"

"No. We've got newspaper from Frank though. I once read that wadded up newspaper worked just fine for cleaning windows."

I went in the bathroom and got the window cleaner, while Becky grudgingly crumpled several sheets of newspaper.

"Ready?" I wasn't sure whether she'd hold onto me or push me out the window.

"Okay. Let's get it over with. I want to go back to bed."

I opened the window and somehow managed to get my shoulders and torso outside but facing in. Sitting with the window down almost to my lap, I was ready. "Okay. Hand me the stuff and hang onto my legs and don't you dare let go."

I sprayed and wiped ever so slowly. No sudden moves—after all we were on the second floor. I had about three fourths of the window finished when a spotlight shone on me.

"Put your hands in the air and don't move."

"Hell. If I put my hands in the air, I'll move—straight down. Who are you?"

"The better question is who are you? I have friends in that room and you will not move any further into that window. Understand me?"

"Deputy. Is that you? This is Linda." I tried to see over my shoulder but the light blinded me.

The light swept downward. "What on earth are you doing? I thought somebody was breaking into your room." He was yelling at me.

"Deputy, I finally thought of a way to clean the outside of this window for Frank. It was the final part of fixing up our room for him. Can I get off this window ledge now?"

"Yes. But the two of you come down here and talk to me." I had a feeling this was not going to be pleasant.

Becky was not amused. I was embarrassed and a little afraid I might be in trouble. *Jesus, don't let my last night here be a headline tomorrow.* "Town heroine cleared of murder charges, but spends night in jail."

We crept down the steps in our bathrobes and slippers. The deputy had already seen my butt hanging out of the window—no dignity left to lose on my part. Becky just didn't care how she looked.

When we stepped out into the black night, the deputy turned on a flashlight so we could see him and he could see us. "Ladies, I turned a blind eye to your drinking and driving. I even began to come by here every night to check on things. Frank was a little worried about two women traveling alone. Imagine how I felt when I thought somebody was climbing in your window. Scared the be'jezus out of me."

"Officer I can't tell you how sorry I am. I wanted to put the finishing touches on a favor for Frank. Never thought about how it would look to somebody driving by. It seems like I've been doing something embarrassing every time I've seen you."

Becky was just standing there. I would have stood up for her, but she was just watching.

"So what should I do ladies? Should I write up a ticket of some kind? Should I fine you to teach you to be more sensible? What should I do? It's not breaking and entering—it's more like opening and exiting. You could have hurt yourself. I don't know how to write this up." He was not amused.

"How about not writing it up at all? We didn't do anything wrong. It may have been stupid, and it scared you, for which I am truly sorry. But it wasn't bad."

The deputy looked at me once again with a cross between amusement and disdain. "Honestly, Linda. For a woman who comes up with such great ideas, you do some dumb things. Don't you know you could have fallen?"

"No, I couldn't. Becky was hanging onto both my legs inside."

He turned to my silent partner. "So you were an accomplice in all this?"

"An unwilling accomplice. I just wanted to get back in bed and sleep. Frankly, I gave serious thought to letting go of those legs."

I was going to kill her tomorrow. I swear I would run her over with my car.

"Okay, ladies. Once again, I am not going to do anything. Mostly because there isn't anything I can do. You weren't breaking any laws—I guess. But I'd really like to think you'd use your heads on the rest of your trip—or at least take turns using your head a little more. That was dangerous. I want you two to come back through here in a few weeks still alive and able bodied."

"Deputy, I will never do another stupid thing in your county. I promise." My fingers were breaking from trying to cross them—even trying to cross my toes in my slippers.

"I'll depend on that ladies." He tipped his hat and started for his patrol car.

"Could we just keep this between us? I really am embarrassed. Especially after the nice honor the town gave us tonight."

"As long as you don't do anything else before you leave, I'll keep it to myself. Good night, ladies. And lock your door. I'll wait to see your light go on and off before I leave."

"Thank you so much. You are too good to us."

We got to the room in record time and turned the light on and off three times, so the deputy would know we were safe. He really was thoughtful, and I didn't even know his name. I felt kind of bad for scaring him, but at least the window was clean.

Becky started dressing and packing last minute things.

"What are you doing? Go back to bed."

"No. By God, you woke me up and almost got us in trouble and then you promised not to do anything else stupid while we're here. The only way we can be sure of keeping that promise is to leave. So get your stuff and let's go. We've told Doug and Jake good-bye and we'll leave Frank a note and payment for this extra week."

I did as I was told. We tidied up the room, dressed, and snuck down the steps quietly.

About fifty miles down the road, Becky had cooled off and we were talking again. I was glad—I hated it when she was angry with me. But we'd been friends for too long to let one of my shenanigans ruin it.

"I'm ready for breakfast. How about you?" Food always made Becky feel better so I knew that would finish her snit.

"What will we find open at this awful hour? "

"Surely there's an all night diner somewhere."

"Full of horny truckers. Are you sure you want to go there? Can you wait until later? We've got some cookies in the back seat."

Becky took off her seat belt and got on her knees to reach back and find the cookies. I hoped I wouldn't have to stop suddenly.

"These will tide us over. What kind do you want?" She opened the box to investigate.

"Any kind. They were all good." No need in being picky now.

She handed me an M & M cookie. "M & M cookies remind me of home. I make these with Matthew and Melinda all the time. I tell them the M's stand for Matthew and Melinda. They love them. Mandy fusses about it but they have to have treats once in a while."

"That's what's so great about grandparenting. We don't have to suffer the consequences of our actions."

"We seem to be pretty good at skipping the consequences of our actions these days." I watched out of the corner of my eye to see if she smiled. "Have you talked to Sonya in the last few days?"

"No. I should call her. We were just so busy and having such a good time and then accused of murder. Didn't seem like a good time to call."

"Not calling is good, don't you think? She needs to let you go and stop clinging to you and you need to get on with living your own life." After a little reflection, I continued. "I'm glad we took this trip. You needed to get away from Sonya and maybe she will learn you can survive without her constant reminders. And I sure as hell needed some time away from Mandy."

"Well, old habits do die hard. Have you heard from Mandy?"

"I had a message on the cell yesterday. I'll call her tonight probably. I've talked to her this week, and it was a pleasant conversation."

"I think she's missing you and just doesn't quite know how to say that." She continued after a pause to finish her cookie. "Do you think we'll get all the way to Branson today?"

"I don't know how far it is. When we stop for breakfast, I'll ask."

For a while, we rode with just the sound of crunching cookies and crumbs being swept off our clothing and the lonely hum of tires on asphalt. Traffic began to pick up, so I figured we were getting close to a town of some kind. Any place we stopped to eat would lose in comparison to the City Café in Eddyville.

I spotted an all night diner as we entered the edge of a small town. The dining room was populated by some hardy early birds—truckers, farmers, and people getting off the night shift. We had our pick of places to sit, and we chose to sit by the windows so we could watch the comings and goings.

"I'm going to order something different today. Maybe pancakes and sausage. This is a trip devoted to change after all."

"Well, Linda, that is a really big change. I'm proud of you. Makes the whole trip worth it."

The waitress walked up to take our order and interrupted this exchange—thank God.

"What'll you have today?" She gave me a weary smile when she asked.

"I'll have apple pancakes, coffee, and link sausage, please."

"And you, ma'am?"

"Sausage, eggs, and all the fixings."

"How do you want those eggs?"

"Sunny side up—to match my mood."

The waitress walked back toward the kitchen slowly and favoring one foot. I could sympathize with that. Waitressing, I had discovered, is hard on the feet.

"You didn't ask about Branson. I hope they have gambling." She might make fun of me for looking for a painting worth millions, but she really thought she could hit it big in a casino. I'm thinking my odds were better than hers.

"I'll ask when the food comes. I want to find out the best route for getting there, too. If they don't have gambling, do you want to go anyway?"

"Maybe. They do have a lot of singers and shows. Course they're mostly over-the-hill stars. I'm not too sure that would be fun. It makes me think about things I'd rather not think about."

"What do you mean?"

"I don't know. Those old timers still trying to sing like they used to seem kind of sad. I think people have to make accommodations for their age, sooner or later." She looked at me. "Do you think we ever look like fools out here chasing fun?"

I thought for a minute. "Well, maybe when I was hanging out that window. Or when you threw that thigh high across the parking lot. But I'd rather look like a fool than be called an old geezerette."

"Me too. Maybe we won't ever have to act our age. Maybe we'll both die in the middle of great sex with a younger man. That would be two different younger men—not a threesome."

Thank you, God. Becky was back. "Well. We never have fit a mold. Why should we start now?"

Breakfast arrived, and we became preoccupied. When the waitress returned to take our plates, I asked about Branson. "How far are we from Branson?"

"It's only about a hundred miles or so."

"Does Branson have casinos?"

"No, ma'am. They have lots of theaters and real good shows but no gambling." This was clearly a well-trained waitress, following the rule, 'Be nice and helpful to customers no matter how tired you are or how much your feet hurt'.

Becky took over the conversation from there. "What is the nearest place with casinos? I want to play the slots on this trip."

"I'm not sure. I'll ask Herbie in the kitchen. He's quite a gambler. I'll find out before I bring your bill." She went in the direction of the kitchen looking for High Roller Herbie.

Becky was a step ahead of the waitress. "I think there's a casino somewhere in southern Illinois. And there's always Tunica. Which way should we go?"

"Let's wait and see if there are any others the gambler in the kitchen knows about. Tunica is a long way from here. What do you know about the Illinois casino?"

"Only that lots of people go there from middle Tennessee. I'm not sure it's a very nice casino, but it has tons of slot machines and that's what I'm looking for."

"How did you get so hung up on playing the slots?"

"It just seems like such easy money. The scenery is probably pretty good in a casino too. Maybe not in the Illinois one though."

"Maybe we'll find those two younger men there—right after **they** hit the jackpot."

We smiled at that thought.

Just then, the waitress walked back. "Herbie says the nearest one is in Metropolis, Illinois, and there is a good one in Tunica, Mississippi."

"Thank you so much for going to all that trouble. We'll have to draw straws or something to decide."

Becky left a generous tip for the waitress, and we made our exit. The day was glorious—one of those sunny days with the mid-western blue sky that looked higher than the heavens. It was a shame to spend it in the car, but we couldn't find a slot machine any other way.

"Okay. Which direction? North to Illinois or south to Tunica?"

"Let's go to Tunica. We can talk on the way. We haven't had a lot of talking time the past week."

"Consider it done. Now help me find a place to buy a map. I wish I had one of those GPS systems."

"Me too. Then you'd hush about a map."

"Well, how do you propose that we find our way to Tunica?"

"Ask directions?"

"What if the person I ask has no idea how to get there?"

"My best guess is they'd say, 'Sorry, ma'am, I don't know.' Honestly, Linda, sometimes you just don't have any common sense."

"Just humor me and let's buy a map."

Pulling into a nearby filling station, Becky pumped the gas and I went looking for a map. The woman inside was reading a gossip magazine and didn't even look up when I opened the door. Good thing I wasn't an armed robber.

"Excuse me, but do you have a map of this part of the country? We're trying to get to Tunica, Mississippi, and I don't know how to get there."

She turned a page before grunting an answer. "Maps on the back wall on the left."

Just past the Twinkies and Little Debby oatmeal cakes, there was a small section of maps. Missouri, Arkansas, Alabama, Georgia, Tennessee, and finally Mississippi. Turns out, I needed a map of the southeastern states. Looking back toward the counter, I could see there was not going to be any assistance forthcoming so I picked up a map of Arkansas and Mississippi. I figured we could find our way using one or both of those.

Becky came in to pay, and I put the maps down on the counter in front of her. She rolled her eyes and didn't ask why I had two maps.

As I started toward the door, Becky went to the bathroom. Knowing her fetish for clean hands, I had a few minutes. I found some money in my purse and bought Little Debby cakes to surprise her when she got hungry.

I sat in the car looking at the maps. A magic marker or highlighter would have been helpful. It was hard to follow the route on those maps. Maybe my prescription sunglasses would help. I was leaning over picking my way through a lot of stuff in a tote bag when Becky came out.

"Now there's a sight. The temptation to kick your butt is about to win over my sense of proper behavior."

"Hah! What sense of proper behavior?"

I put my sunglasses on and got back in the driver's seat while Becky buckled herself up ready to find some slot machines. She looked over and noticed my sunglasses.

"Are those Gucci's?" There was a mix of surprise and dismay in her voice.

"Yeah. I bought these the same day I bought those wonderful lizard skin boots. Don't you want to put your sunglasses on? It's going to be really sunny today."

For once Becky didn't argue. She put on some bright green plastic sunglasses. "Mine are more hoochie than Gucci." She flipped the mirror down to look at herself. "Hey, we can be the hoochie, Gucci girls in Tunica."

It was good to be on our way and both in a better mood.

We drove south on state Highway 61. The day was one of those last gasps of summer that September brings. Certain leaves were showing signs of color, but mostly things were still green. The tobacco farmers were busy skewering stalks on pointed stakes. Hay lay in fields in huge rolls waiting for the winter. There was an air of both expectation and resignation among farmers this time of year. I remembered it well from my childhood. The price of tobacco determined what I got for Christmas each year. The hay might last through the winter, or it might get wet and rot. Sort of like my life—so much was not in my control, it seemed.

Becky looked over and interrupted my reverie. "Are you missing home and the kids and grandkids?"

"You know, I am beginning to miss them. Lord knows we needed to get away, and I've had a ball, but I'm beginning to think about home more often."

"Maybe that's why most vacations last two or three weeks. I'm missing Sonya and the kids, too. Sonya drives me crazy, but I know she loves me. She wants to take care of me, but she was becoming the problem instead of the solution. I worry that when I die she won't be able to cope."

"Don't you think all people our age begin to think about things like that? My fear is that when I die, Mandy won't be able to live with her sense of guilt for the last few years."

"That's a legitimate concern. But she also knows you love her and that includes seeing beyond mistakes. I'm sure you've made a few of those, too. I think she's begun to miss you and maybe appreciate you more."

"I can't tell. She calls regularly, and I really had not expected that."

"So Mandy is paying more attention to your absence than you had expected, and Sonya is calling less. Maybe they're learning what they needed to learn while we're out having fun. After all, we've been gone almost a month."

"Yeah. I am beginning to miss home. How much longer do you think we should be gone?"

"Well, we spent a lot of our earnings in Eddyville re-doing our room at Frank's Place. I'd say we could probably last another week or ten days, if we can find some more part-time work. What do you think?'

"Maybe. We can't work in Tunica. I think they're pretty careful about hiring in casinos. And I don't want to go home without spending a few days in the mountains. We could probably get some kind of work there."

"Okay. Let's spend two nights in Tunica, three nights in the mountains, and one or two nights in Eddyville on the way home. That should put us back in Millerton in another week." My God, Becky really was beginning to plan!

"Sounds like a plan. And let's start calling the girls every night. I really want us both to go home to better relationships." I was quiet for a minute before continuing. "I'm proud of us. We took things in our own hands, had an adventure, and at the same time may have improved things at home. We're pretty damn good."

"Well, of course. Didn't you know that? We're unorthodox but brilliant!"

We drove on thinking our private thoughts for a while. I suspect it was a good thing we both had on sunglasses. Neither of us wanted the other to see our tearing up, as we thought about home and aging and what the future held for us. I remembered something Becky said the day before and decided to pursue the discussion a bit more. "Remember when we were talking about the old singers in Branson looking foolish? Honestly, do you think we are looking foolish to people?"

"Maybe to some. Seems to me there is a difference in foolish and fun. We aren't taking stupid risks or running from responsibilities. We aren't having tummy tucks and boob jobs trying to look younger. We're just out here trying to add some fun and adventure to our humdrum lives. What's foolish about that?"

"I guess I still worry too much about how things look to people. That's one of the ways you're good for me—you remind me not to do that so much. You're right—we're just trying to liven up our routine. Wonder why some people think that's foolish for people our age?"

"Probably because they're bored and don't have the guts to do anything about it." She did know how to cut to the chase.

We drove on, lost in silence. Mouthy as we were, silence was comfortable too. Becky kept things lively and funny, and I was usually working on a plan of some kind, but we both also knew when to be quiet. This was one of those times.

When the digital clock on the dash said 12:00, I started watching for a nice restaurant that might have a clean bathroom. I thought I saw a sign for an Applebee's up ahead. Not gourmet but usually good.

"Get your glasses out of the glove box and see if that sign says there is an Applebee's up ahead."

Becky tried squinting to see. When that didn't work, she got her glasses. "Yeah, and I think I see it up ahead on the right. Wouldn't want you to have to make a left turn!"

"Why, thank you, my friend."

I turned the car into the parking lot and found a spot near the door. Inside, Becky got us a table while I went to the bathroom. First things first. When I returned, Becky already knew what she wanted and asked me to order for her while she used the facilities. I noticed her checking her purse for her cleaning supplies—some things had not changed.

The waitress had that clean-cut Midwestern look. She spoke with just a hint of a twang. "What can I get for you?'

"I want your grilled chicken sandwich, and my friend wants the oriental salad—with extra dressing. Sweet tea for both of us."

"I'll get that tea for you right now."

"Thank you."

Becky came back—with very clean hands, I'm sure—and we began to talk about the children again.

The worry lines between her eyes told me she was in a serious mode. "When we start calling them more often, maybe we can work up to the things that worry us with the kids. It would be great to go home with some different ground rules."

"What do you think are good ground rules for adult children and parents?" I valued her opinions and ideas. We had seen each other through every step of life—marriage, parenthood, and now widowhood. Even through finding new boyfriends.

"You're the social worker. What do you think?"

"Being a social worker hasn't helped me with this. I want Mandy to *want* to talk to me and to visit me. I want her to *enjoy* being with me. She doesn't. And when we have a moment of pleasure together, it seems to scare her to death. If I push, it just makes it worse. If I point out how hurt I am, it makes her angry. I don't know what to do."

"Maybe Mandy has to fix this herself. Maybe you can't make it okay. So far as I can see, you aren't the problem—Mandy is. Taking a vacation from each other is exactly what you needed to do. The ball is in her court. You're out having a good time, and she must have found some other resources for all the things she asks you to do. Maybe when she doesn't need you so much she will begin to want you."

"How did you get so smart, Becky? I think you're a better social worker than I ever was. Let's just keep having fun and begin to call home more often."

Lunch arrived and, as usual, conversation stopped. When we finished eating, we lingered a while over a fresh glass of tea. Something we hadn't done in a while. "I can't tell you how much I've enjoyed getting back to some serious talk. I love your fun side, but right now I need your serious side to help me with Mandy."

"Well, even I can't do fun 24/7. It was time to shift gears. The last few weeks, we had a lot of fun, did a lot of helping folks, and almost got in big time trouble. It was great, but I gotta' tell you—I'm worn out."

"Me too. That's why I fell asleep at 4 o'clock the other day, I guess. I'm tired. Let's take it easy today and stop early. Then we'll call the kids and call it a day. The fun will come back when the time is right. My best guess is it won't be a long time."

"Yeah. We're not the type to be serious too long. Let's get going."

We gathered our purses and paid the bill. Walking out into the gorgeous autumn day, I couldn't help thinking that today was proving to be refreshing in a whole different way.

chapter

TWELVE

After we had been on the road for a while, Becky began squirming around. I knew that meant her back was bothering her. "Let's stop early, and then we'll get to Tunica late tomorrow afternoon?"

"Good idea. We're both tired, and we need to call the girls and have a long talk with them." She began fishing in the glove box for her extra glasses. "I'll start watching for a place to stay."

I noticed she was only looking on the right side of the road. That's one thing I loved about her—she might be prickly, but underneath that she was considerate. She hid it pretty well, but it was there.

"That sign said there was a Holiday Inn up ahead. That's usually reasonable and clean. Want to stop there?"

"Any place is okay with me. If we go in and it's not clean, we'll drive a little further."

I saw the Holiday Inn up ahead. I pulled under the covered driveway, and Becky went in with her credit card to check us in. Waiting in the car, I began to think about what I'd say to Mandy. I couldn't just start in on how excluded she made me feel. Not only would that make her mad, it sounded whiny, and I hated sounding whiny. Maybe I could just talk about who's ferrying Matthew and Melinda around. That might lead into some talk about how much she's missing me or how much she's learned about doing things for herself. I knew I had to take it slow on trying to make things right between us. I'd always been so afraid of having no connection with her that I accepted behaviors I shouldn't accept. In that sense, I was to blame and had to do some changing myself.

Becky opened the car door and motioned for me to drive ahead and to the right. We unloaded our things and walked up the steps. We had decided that steps were healthier than elevators, but by the time I got to the room I wasn't so sure we were right.

Stepping inside, we looked around, and Becky checked out the bathroom. That was the standard of cleanliness for her. "It's clean enough for me. How about you?"

"Believe me; if it's clean enough for you, it is fine for me."

After putting our bags on the luggage racks, we sat in the chairs and stretched out our legs trying to get the kinks out of them. I began holding my legs up and making circles with my feet.

"Why do you do that? I've seen you do it several times."

"It helps loosen up the muscles and get the blood circulating again. Try it."

I picked up the cell phone and checked my watch. I knew the children would be home from school, but Mandy would still be working.

"I think I'll call the grandkids. They'll let me know what's going on. What do you think?"

"Good idea. Then you can call Mandy later." Becky chose her next words carefully. "And when you talk to her, take it slow, Linda. I think she has a hard time talking about how she feels and an even harder time saying she's wrong. Just let the conversation go wherever it goes. You can't fix what you didn't break, but you might want to make it easy for her to fix it. Do you know what I mean?"

"I know. But I am terrified that I won't live long enough for her to decide to do that."

"Why do you say that? Is there anything wrong?"

"No. But I am sixty-seven years old. By this time, you'd think the mother-daughter thing would be worked out. And anybody my age can develop health problems. Any of us can be snuffed out like a candle. Even a twenty five year old can drop dead or be killed in an accident."

"Lord, you are worried. Are you sure you don't have any health problems you haven't told me about?"

"Not really. I have an irregular heartbeat every now and then, but the doctor didn't find anything wrong. I guess those episodes have scared me though."

"Well, we're going to take it slow and easy from now on, and when you decide it's time to go home we will. Now call the kids and find out what's happening at home."

"I think I'll go out on the little balcony. I'll probably get better reception out there."

On the second ring, Matthew answered. "Gran, is that you?"

"Yeah. How's my buddy?"

"Fine. We won our football game today. I wish you could have seen me. I made the winning touchdown."

"Oh, I wish I could have seen that, too. Who took you to the game?"

"Johnny's mother has been taking us to practice and games since you've been gone. She doesn't make M & M cookies for us, but she's pretty cool."

"I'm glad. Does she make you wear your seatbelt?" I was obsessive about seatbelts.

"Oh, yeah. She won't even start the car until we're all buckled in. Worse than you are, Gran."

"What's Melinda up to?"

"Same old girly stuff. She's been hanging out with Gracey Coles. They spend hours playing dress-up. That box of old clothes you gave her hasn't been put away since you left—she finally took it to Gracey's house."

"Is she there now? Could I talk to her too?"

"I think she's up in her room. I'll yell for her."

"Matt, do you have the doors locked like you're supposed to?"

"We've done all the things Mama told us to do, and Mrs. Bradley is always home next door if we need anything. We're fine. Are you having fun?"

"Yes. Becky and I are having a good time. Beginning to miss all of you though." I didn't think he needed to know his grandmother had been suspected of murder.

"When will you be home? We miss you too. Even Mom misses you. She said so the other day."

"I'll be home in about a week. I'm anxious to see everybody. Now put Melinda on the phone for a minute. I don't want to run out of minutes on this phone."

"Okay. I hope you're home in time to see some of my ball games."

"I will be, honey. Gran loves you. Take care of yourself."

I could hear Matthew yelling for his sister to come to the phone. "It's Gran. Hurry up. She's running out of minutes."

Clomp, clomp, clomp. Down the stairs she came.

"Gran. Where are you?"

"Well, we're headed from Missouri to Mississippi right now. We'll be home in about another week. What are you up to while I'm gone?"

"School of course. Ugh. Gracey and I have been getting together after school at her house. We have lots of fun. And Mama is home a lot more on the weekends lately and that's nice. She's actually making M & M cookies for us. They're not as good as yours, but I don't tell her that. It would hurt her feelings."

"I'm glad you don't tell her that. How is your mother?"

"She's okay. I think she wants you to come home though. She's a lot busier since you've been gone. But I like having her home more. I don't mean to hurt your feelings, Gran. I love being with you, too."

"Oh, honey. You won't hurt my feelings. I'm glad you're having more time with your mother. That's important. And you know what? I needed some time for myself with my friend, too. I hope that doesn't hurt your feelings."

"No, Gran. I think Aunt Becky is cool, and I'll bet you guys are having lots of fun."

"We are. Tell your mom I'll call her tonight. I was just thinking about you and Matthew and decided to call early and talk to you. Tell your mom we'll talk tonight."

"Okay, Gran. I love you."

"Me too, sweetie."

I hit the 'end' button and went inside, where Becky was just finishing a conversation with Sonya.

"How did it go with Sonya?"

"Good actually. She didn't ask about my health once, and that's a huge change. How were Matt and Melinda?"

"Adorable, as always. They miss me. They said their mother did too. Do you think that's possible?"

"Sure it is. This is the first time you've been away from her for very long. I'm sure she misses you—and not just what you do for her."

"Well, I'm glad you're so sure. I'm not. I'm not going to do so much for her any more. It is time to call a halt to that."

"Do you think you can make that stick when you get home?"

"I hope so. There's a lot at stake here. Time with my grandchildren and a relationship with my daughter for openers. At least when she was using me, I was also in contact. I hope I can change."

"Linda, you are going to have to change. It isn't working if your goal is a good relationship with Mandy. And you can't keep doing as much as you've been doing. We are, much as I hate to admit it, getting older."

"Well, thank you for that! But, I know you're right. And that fact is probably the basis of Sonya's concern for you. She's afraid you're going to die prematurely, I think. Strange—those of us approaching the age to concern ourselves with death are not the ones worrying."

"And you know what? We are not going to start now. After you talk to Mandy tonight, we are getting back to our little adventure. But you have to promise me one thing. If you begin to feel bad, you'll tell me. Promise?"

"I promise. I swear, the doctor saw no problem with my heart. He thought maybe I was just overstressed."

"Then I guess we'd better stop nearly getting arrested."

"I guess. I didn't mind the almost DUI or breaking and entering, but I sure as hell got stressed over the murder thing. I hope we find out what happened to poor old Earl when we go back through Eddyville."

"Yeah. Me too. And, I don't know about you, but I have no intention of telling the kids about that little episode."

"God, no. I don't even want to think what would happen if they knew about that. They'd probably have us declared incompetent and send us to the old folks funny farm."

The next morning we loaded the car and were ready to leave by eight o'clock. We both felt better after talking to the grandchildren, and my conversation with Mandy had been very pleasant.

"Let's get going to the slot machines." Becky's eyes twinkled with excitement and she walked out with an attitude.

"Watch out, Tunica. Here come the hoochy, Gucci girls from Tennessee." I pulled out into traffic and we were off. This time I didn't burst into song; I just hummed quietly. I could have sworn I heard Becky humming too.

We pulled into Tunica about four o'clock that afternoon. After looking at some brochures, we had decided to stay at the Strike Gold Casino. She thought the name was an indicator of how our visit would turn out. Talk about a positive thinker!

After a few wrong turns—even Mapquest didn't always get it right—we pulled under the covered entry. A bellhop immediately came over to get our bags. Oh, how I did like being waited on. This place was going to be more to my liking than Frank's Place and almost as cheap.

I popped the trunk, and Becky and the bellman got our bags and went to check us in. Another eager, gum-chewing young man appeared at the driver side of the car. "Ya'll want me to park your car?" His over-sized sunglasses were a throwback to the eighties, I thought, but around here, you might need big shades.

"Why, yes. That would be nice. We won't be taking it out again until we leave day after tomorrow." I handed him the valet key and reached over to get Becky's glasses out of the glove box. Before I walked away, I looked in the back seat and noticed our stash of liquor. *Maybe I'd better take that with me. Wouldn't want the valet to tie one on and wreck my car.* With my purse on my shoulder, I was able to carry the Black Jack and Beefeaters safely.

The interior was more impressive than I expected. Crystal chandeliers and marble floors made me think I was paying a lot more than fifty-nine dollars a night—and I would be by the time we finished with the slot machines.

The bellhop and Becky were waiting for me at the elevators. We zipped up to the eleventh floor—odd there was no thirteenth floor shown on the key pad.

"Why is there no thirteenth floor?"

The young man with the luggage carrier smiled. "The number thirteen is unlucky. Don't want you to be unlucky here."

Yeah. Right, I thought. But for once, I kept my thoughts to myself.

The high-pitched ding signaled our arrival at the eleventh floor. After going in the room and tipping the bellhop, we surveyed our surroundings with pleasure. Clean, well decorated, and two queen-sized beds.

"I think we've moved uptown."

"Yeah, and when I hit it big we'll move even more uptown. Ready to go down and try our hand at the slots?"

"Isn't it a little early?"

"Oh, no. Casinos have gambling 24/7. Let's get started, then have dinner, and we'll call it a night early. How's that?"

Becky knew more than I did about casinos. She found the window where she could get some tokens and we were good to go. I got ten dollars worth of tokens, and she put twenty dollars worth on her credit card. After walking just a short distance, she decided that big cup of tokens was too heavy. She poured half of them in her purse.

"I hope you don't get scoliosis from that purse."

"Don't worry. I'm going to win enough to hire somebody to haul it around for me."

"I hope."

We walked around the slot machine area looking for just the right spot. I didn't care, but Becky thought it mattered. She pointed to her left. "Here's the spot. This has good karma."

"Are you sure? Look at that woman. Those stretched to the limit spandex stirrup pants and that belly-hiding Hawaiian shirt don't say good karma to me. And that brassy dye job is horrendous." I squinted to get a better look. "What is that all over her purse?"

Becky noticed her for the first time. "Jesus, she must have twenty-five pictures stuck in those see through plastic pockets on that purse. We will definitely get the prize for classiness on this row of machines."

We sat several spaces down from this woman. She was playing the hell out of that slot machine. Going just as fast as she could—no telling how many tokens she put in that thing.

We started slow, and I just hoped to break even by the end of the night. Becky was still convinced she was going to get a jackpot. It did get a little addictive watching to see if maybe the next time I'd see three of something on that screen. I never did, but every now and then, I'd get two with a small payoff. Becky was getting absolutely nothing.

The tacky woman picked up her purse and left and Becky decided to move down to her machine.

"Why are you moving?"

"Well, I figure she's been playing that same machine for a long time, and that makes my odds better."

Becky put in a token, raised her eyes to the heavens in prayer, and slowly pulled the lever down. I have never heard such a racket in my life. Lights and sirens were going off, and the coins just kept falling down into that tray. Just as the tray was about to overflow onto the floor, a man who worked for the casino came over to help us.

"Wow. You are one lucky lady. Nobody has hit a jackpot like this one all day. You're going to get at least a thousand dollars here."

"Oh, my God." Becky was practically twirling around in excitement. "I told you I'd hit it big. I told you."

As the casino staffer finished gathering up the coins, the woman who had just left that machine came back. She stood with her mouth hanging open, and the veins on her forehead popped out. I thought she was going to have a stroke.

She screeched at the casino employee. "That money is mine. I've been playing this machine all afternoon. I stepped away for just a second, and this heifer took my machine and won my money. I want that money." By now, she was shouting so loud that a crowd gathered.

Becky was not about to give up her jackpot. "Whoa. I put in the token that won the money. This money is mine, and don't you even think about trying to take it away from me." She looked her straight in the eye with a withering stare.

The other woman came toward Becky, and I thought she was going to start a catfight right there in front of everybody. Fortunately, the man who came to help us stepped in.

"Ma'am, whoever puts in the winning token gets the money. I'm sorry you're so upset, but the money goes to this lady. How about if I arrange for you to get a free roll of tokens to start over?"

"Like hell. I'll take my business elsewhere." She looked back at Becky in a way that would have made me wet my pants.

Becky took a step toward her and opened her big mouth one more time. "I'll tell you what I'll do. I'll give you a hundred dollars if you promise to get rid of that God awful purse." The young man could hardly contain her this time. He set the bucket of quarters down so he would have both hands available. By now, onlookers were taking sides in all this, and I was afraid we might start a riot. I was happy to see a guard coming our way.

"Becky, come on. Let's get this money over to the window and get some bills and get out of here." I turned to the young guard and asked him to carry the bucket of quarters for us.

Becky started to say something else, and I gave her my do it and die look. We walked away in the opposite direction from the irate gambler and her casino escort. Just before going out the door, Miss Tacky Personified had to have the last word. "You ain't seen the last of me."

At the window waiting for them to give us bills, I looked over my shoulder to be sure the woman was nowhere around. "Damn, Becky. She scared me to death. I'm not sure we need to stay here tonight— she might come looking for us."

"She was a specimen alright. Surely they won't let her back in here as mad as she was. I don't know, but she is not getting this money."

The girl inside the cage handed Becky five one hundred dollar bills and ten fifties. Becky rolled it up gangster fashion and stuffed it in her bra. If that floosie came looking for the money, it was going to get very personal.

I wanted to get out of the gambling part of the casino. "Want to eat a bite and then go to our room? We were going to turn in early and talk some more, and I think maybe we need to do that now."

"Okay. I'll keep my eye out for that old bat. Lord, she was tacky. Even I care more than that about how I look."

We found The Buffet and were not disappointed. It featured everything we were accustomed to and all we could eat. No wonder people in this country were getting fat.

Just before we went for seconds, I looked across the room and thought I saw someone from Millerton. "Is that Elizabeth? You know the really classy woman that you did some decorating for?"

"I think it is. She once paid me to re-do a bedroom with $400 a yard fabric. I kept hoping she'd decide she didn't like it and do it all over again. But I guess it was exactly what she wanted. I can't believe she's in a place like this. She isn't a bit snobby, but she's so classy. I'd expect her to be in Las Vegas to do her gambling."

About that time, Elizabeth spotted us and walked our way. I could only hope she had not seen the near free for all.

"Hello, Becky. And Linda. I'm surprised to see someone from home. May I join you for a bit?"

"Sure. We were just contemplating going back for seconds."

"Oh, I say go for it. When will any of us cook this kind of meal at home?"

"You like meat-and-three kind of food?" I was shocked for some reason.

"I love it. I get tired of the attempted gourmet stuff. So often people try and miss. Don't tell anyone at home I said that. You know I suffer through a lot of events with people who think they are better cooks than they are." She chuckled more to herself than to us.

Becky responded, "I say we are all a long way from home and can do whatever we want—including going back for seconds." She left the table to do exactly that.

I continued the conversation with Elizabeth. "It's nice to see you. We weren't expecting to find anyone from home here. Do you enjoy gambling?"

"I love it, but I always come by myself. You know my friends think gambling is not a terribly ladylike thing to enjoy."

"Well you just stick with us, and we'll have lots of fun. And what happens in Tunica stays in Tunica."

Becky returned with her food and our conversation continued.

"What do you like to play?" Becky and Elizabeth might be kindred souls.

"I like black jack, and I love the slot machines. I started over that way a while ago, but there was some kind of confrontation going on. I decided to wait and go there later."

Becky and I almost choked. Trying to swallow, instead of inhaling my food while laughing, was a bit problematic. Becky ended up having to cover her mouth with her napkin to keep from spitting her food across the table.

"Was that you two?"

We nodded our heads, with a mixture of amusement and embarrassment. Becky recovered her voice first. "It was. I put in one token and won a thousand dollars and the woman who had been playing that slot all afternoon pitched a fit. They had to show her out. I'm not entirely sure she won't come back looking for me." Becky glanced over her shoulder to emphasize the point.

"You're kidding. Are you really scared of that?"

Unlike Becky, I was happy to admit my concern. "I am. I think we ought to leave and stay somewhere else tonight. What do you think?"

"Does she know your room number?" Clearly, Elizabeth was more level headed than most privileged characters.

"No. So, I guess we're safe." The hotel wouldn't give out our room number. I learned a long time ago at a convention, when some goon was putting the moves on me. That memory had served me well more than once.

"Well, if she sees you going into your room, you can always pack up and come stay in my suite. There's plenty of space."

"Are you sure? We wouldn't want to interfere with your time here."

"Oh, it would be fun to have someone I know around—especially people who don't look down their nose at gambling. So just call me if you need to stay with me."

Becky looked relieved, though she claimed not to be worried. I suspected she would decorate this woman's whole house free of charge the next time she asked.

We finished supper with a final trip to the dessert buffet. When we got up to leave, I turned to Elizabeth and said with a chuckle, "We'll call you, if we need your protection. And thanks a million."

"You are most welcome and when we all get home, let's get together for lunch. I am so happy I ran into you here. I know your kids and grandkids will be glad to have you back home in a few days. I saw Mandy the other day and she mentioned that she was really missing you, Linda."

We went in different directions, Elizabeth to the slot machines and us to our room. I walked toward the elevator shaking my head. "Mandy missing me? I hope that's true."

While Becky was packing her few things for an early departure the next morning, I decided to call home. "I think I'll call Mandy now. I don't have much packing to do and I want to talk to her and let her know where to find us."

"When I finish here, I'll go out on the balcony and call Sonya too. Then we can just relax for the rest of the night."

I dialed Mandy's number and was happy when she picked up quickly.

"Hey, Mom. What are you up to now?"

"We're in Tunica and Becky won $1000 with her first quarter in a slot machine. Can you believe that?"

"My lord. I didn't think that ever happened. What are *you* doing?"

"Mostly I've been trying to keep Becky from getting in a fist fight with the woman who had been playing that slot all day. It was awful at the time, but it's kind of funny now."

"Good grief. When are you two coming home?" With just a brief pause, she continued, "I've gotten your point, Mom and I miss you. I'm not going to depend on you so much from now on."

"Oh, honey. I'm so glad to hear that. I'm really getting too old to do so much and I think you'll enjoy being the one to do a lot of it anyway. Your kids are great fun to be around. I miss them—and I miss you too."

It was a moment before Mandy continued. "When you get back things will be different. I promise."

"Good. How have you arranged everything?"

"Well, Hazel takes care of the kids after school and they ride to practices and lessons with friends. When I can get off early, I take them and I've been to all their after-hours activities since you've been gone. You're right. They are a lot of fun."

"Oh, that makes me happy to hear. We'll be home in less than a week. We're going to leave here tomorrow, a day earlier than planned, and go back through the Ozark Mountains for a day or so. Then we'll stop back in Eddyville for a couple of nights and be home."

"I can hardly wait to hear about your trip. Especially Eddyville. Sounds like you made some friends there. Be careful and call me every day or two."

"I will. And I can hardly wait to see all of you and give you a hug. I'm proud of you, Mandy."

"I love you, Mom. And I'm kind of proud of me too."

Becky came in from the balcony just as I finished and we compared notes.

"How's Sonya?"

"She's fine and so are the kids. And she seems a lot more relaxed. She didn't ask about my health or medications a single time. I think things will be different when we get back."

"Mandy *told* me things were going to be different for us. She finally gets it and I didn't bother to tell her how much it would cost to replace me. The point was to get her to be more independent—not to prove how great I am."

"All right! Life is good. Let's finish off our stash of liquor and get ready for bed."

"Sounds great to me." Now I was as anxious to get back home, as I had been to leave. Life was good indeed.

chapter

THIRTEEN

The next morning, Becky made us reservations at an inn in the Ozarks, while I was loading the car. I knew it was time to get home for some rest—or exercise—when I got out of breathe loading the luggage. I thought I was in better shape than that.

We drove north on a beautiful day. There had been some cool nights and leaves were beginning to show signs of color. The mountains would probably be beautiful.

"You know, I can hardly wait to get to the inn. I think my soul began in the mountains, and I was reincarnated as a small town girl. I'll enjoy just sitting and thinking and talking."

"Me, too. It's time to go home. We're both tired, and I did notice that you get out of breath sometimes. Are you okay?"

"Yes. I'm fine. I haven't exercised in almost a month, and I'm feeling the difference that makes."

"You tell me if you feel bad. I can drive this car safely. You don't have to do all of it."

"I may let you drive a while after lunch. That way I can look at the scenery as we come into the mountains."

"That's a deal."

We drove on thinking our own thoughts. I was remembering my last conversation with Mandy. My heart soared when I thought about the difference between our first conversation on this trip and last night's conversation. I really wanted to get home and give her a hug and then make cookies with the grandkids. I suspected Becky was feeling much the same way.

After a quick stop for lunch, I gave the car keys to Becky and piled in the passenger seat. It was a relief to be off duty as the driver. I was more tired than I realized.

"I'll be careful, Linda. Now you relax and watch the world go by."

"Happily. Maybe I'm getting old after all. What do you think qualifies for old?"

"When you stop enjoying life, you are old. We are not there yet."

"Whew. I'm relieved. I don't mind needing to rest, but I hate the thought of being an old woman."

Becky pretended to be concentrating on her driving. After a minute, she asked, "What do you hate about that? I know what I hate, but what do you hate?"

"Not being able to do things I enjoy. Not being able to physically do all the things I'm used to doing."

"Same here. But even worse is the thought of not being able to use my mind. People see me as just wanting to have a good time. That's true, but I want to do it on my terms, and that involves thinking and being able to carry off spontaneous activity, as well as making plans. I don't want to live without a good enough mind to do that."

We drove in silence for a while. Those were heavy thoughts for a couple of rowdy women in their late sixties out to have an adventure, I thought. But honest thoughts. Getting old was scary.

I looked over toward Becky. "Maybe it's losing control of what happens and how it's dealt with that scares us both."

"Do you think it's time to have that dreaded end of life discussion with our kids?"

"Maybe. Let's talk about this some more tonight."

I leaned my head back to think. The next thing I knew, we were pulling into the inn.

It was a two story stone building that receded into a hillside. The grey stone made the perfect backdrop for ivy and rhododendron. It faced a gorgeous range of mountains. Becky had reserved adjoining rooms for us. We could see the mountains from inside our rooms or out on the balcony. As the sun set, the picture before us changed in subtle and colorful ways. The wondrous swirl of nature, I thought.

We settled into lounge chairs on my balcony. I spoke first. "Isn't this gorgeous? A perfect spot—at the foot of mountains watching the approach of twilight."

Becky held a glass with the last drop of her Beefeaters. "I can't think of a better way to end our journey. I almost wish we hadn't promised to stop back in Eddyville."

"Me, too. But we did, and we'd feel bad if we didn't do it. After all, we promised to cook for the senior center. I'm looking forward to seeing everybody again. Especially Jake. "

I could almost hear Becky snap to attention. "I know I'm looking forward to seeing Doug again. I think you already knew that though."

"You two are not terribly subtle." I continued watching the changing sky, as I laughed quietly about her lack of subtlety.

"Do you think we could actually tolerate a man in our lives after so many years of widowhood?"

I thought about that before answering. "I'm not sure. I'd certainly enjoy an occasional roll in the hay, but I'm not sure I want to marry again." Then I decided to be more honest. "And I'm still holding out on that roll in the hay. I talk big, but having casual sex is just not my style. I wish it was—I might have had a lot more fun the last few years."

"I handle the casual roll in the hay just fine. But I would enjoy a long, monogamous relationship, too." She looked toward the mountains as she spoke. We were both making confessions that went against our public personas.

We watched the sky turn from blue to pink to purple to gray. Not unlike our lives, I thought. Always changing color and hue.

"I hope it works out for you and Doug. He's a nice man, and you obviously like him."

"I do. We're not too old you know."

"I know. Maybe just too scared?"

When it became fully dark, we went inside to dress for dinner. We both felt rested and, for the first time in a while, took extra care with our appearance. That was a good sign of the value of this trip.

In the dining room, we looked at the menu and decided to throw all the nutrition rules out for the night. I ordered a steak and all the trimmings, and Becky ordered trout with drawn butter. Sonya would have had a fit at the butter.

Becky looked at me with an unusually serious expression. "Today has really been nice. I love that I have you to talk with and confide in."

"Me, too." After a brief pause, I responded with a question I had been thinking about. "Tell me—what is the happiest day of your life?"

"No question—the day I married Charlie. How about you?"

"No doubt—the last conversation I had with Mandy. I have yearned for that conversation. It was like manna from heaven."

"This trip was the best decision we've made in a while." Becky thought for a time before continuing. "Which do you think is the real 'us'—tonight or the night we almost got a DUI?" Her smile mixed with an expression of real curiosity.

"They're both us. We've just come to the time in life when the "DUI us" won't show up as often, I think. Or at least it shouldn't."

"And that is a part of aging I don't like. I'm not anxious to get a DUI, but I'm not ready to say good-bye to the rowdy part of us either."

The waitress brought our salads just then, and we were quiet for a while. The salads were fresh and crisp and had those extras that made them special—walnuts, cranberries, crumbled goat cheese. Our reflective day spilled over into enjoying each bite of food.

Putting my plate over to the side for the waitress, I picked up the conversation where we left it. "Being more calm and thoughtful is feeling good to me. Zany takes a lot of energy, and I don't have as much of that as I used to have."

"Are you sure you're okay? You have been awfully tired the last day or two."

"I think I'm fine. Hearing Mandy say the things she said to me last night was like ending a long war. I think for the first time in years, I am able to relax."

"I know what you mean. Taking off and having a few weeks of fun was just what I needed. Now that I've done that, I'm ready to go back. Clearly, this journey has been more than geographical."

Our entrees arrived and as with the salads, we took our time and savored each bite.

"How many nights did you reserve here?"

"Only tonight. I'm thinking we both want to get home. Do you want to stay longer?"

"No, but I'd like us to come back here sometime. Maybe Jake and Doug could meet us for a weekend sometime."

"That sounds wonderful." There was that incorrigible glint in her eye.

"Who'd have thought this trip would end up with two old friends coming to terms with their children and their age? *And* finding two interesting male companions. I never expected any of those things quite honestly."

"Like I said before—we make quite a team. Do you want to splurge and get a dessert?"

"Yes. Something totally decadent. Chocolate, of course."

The waitress went over their dessert selections and we both ordered something called a chocolate volcano. I was not entirely sure what that was, but I was certain it was appropriately indulgent.

Armed with both a fork and a spoon, we discovered that the dessert was exactly what it sounded like—a mound of cake with a chocolate truffle interior that was the consistency of lava. We did not waste time talking during this exercise in indulgence. Just some oooing and ahhing. It sounded a little like good sex sounds.

When we returned to the room, I dug out my two miniature bottles of Black Jack that I kept in reserve. On the deck, it was cool enough for a sweater, but warm enough to be pleasant. A rising moon outlined the mountains against the sky. There was no need to talk. This is a coming home moment, I thought. My heart filled with the joy of it and the contentment which had been absent for so long. Maybe that is what good aging is—coming to terms and being at peace. I had accomplished both on this trip.

Becky's face told me she was experiencing some of the same feelings. We had been friends so long; we read each other's aura with amazing accuracy. She looked at me and then reached over and took my hand. "I love you, Linda. I don't know what my life would have been without you, but I'm glad I have not had to learn that lesson."

I patted her hand. "I love you, too. I can't imagine a life without you. You have always been there—for laughing and crying. And for yelling at me or listening to me. And for getting me out of more than a few scrapes. You are my sister, in the real sense of the word."

"And I'm proud to be your sister." She withdrew her hand. "Let's turn in before we get totally maudlin. We'll get an early start tomorrow. What do you say?"

"I say, let's do exactly that."

We gathered our glasses and pulled ourselves out of the lounge chairs. Before going inside, we gave each other a hug. It had been a special evening.

***

The next day we drove into Frank's parking lot right after lunch. Just as we walked in the front door, Frank came out from the back. "Well, look who's here! Tubby and I were wondering today when you'd be back."

"We're glad to be back. How is everyone?" I set my bag down as I spoke.

"We're all about the same. All your projects are up and running. Ya'll want the same room. Or maybe you'd like a different room and you can decorate another one?" Frank displayed that half smile we saw before.

"Not this time Frank. Maybe next time." Becky might see this as a bargaining opportunity for the future.

"Here's the key. I'll call and let the people at the center know you're here. You promised to cook supper for us, you know."

"Yep. We have it all planned and can hardly wait to see our friends."
We didn't quite have it planned, but we'd work on that in the next hour.

Inside the room, Becky practically dove for the phone. While she talked to Doug, I started my shower. Neither of us wanted to waste any time getting over to the center.

An hour later, as we went out the front door, Frank called for us to wait up. He looked nervous and serious, so we went right back inside. I hoped there was not more trouble about Earl's death.

"Girls, I've been thinking while you were gone. I'm about ready to slow down and semi-retire. Would you all be interested in moving here and helping me run this place?"

I don't know about Becky, but I was stunned. Frank was so private, and this place seemed to be his whole life.

Becky was never stunned into speechlessness. "What do you have in mind, Frank?"

"Well. What I was thinking was that I could make part of the place private living quarters for you two, and you could re-decorate the whole place—on a budget of course. Then we could share duties at the desk. I couldn't pay you much, but you'd have free living space and utilities."

"Frank, that sounds like a really good idea. Could we have time to talk about it and talk it over with our children? We should be able to give you an answer in a couple of weeks." I found myself excited at this new twist, but I did not want to jeopardize the situation with Mandy.

Becky was on speed dial again. "Frank, I am already measuring windows for curtains—in my mind, at least. Are you sure you want to do this?"

"I've thought a lot about it while you've been gone. I talked to Tubby and some others, and they all think it's a good idea. This town needs you two and missed you after you left—some more than others. I hope you'll say yes."

"We're flattered that you would offer this to us, Frank. And we'll give you an answer as soon as possible. We need to get going now. You're coming to the center for supper I hope."

"Wouldn't miss it. Be careful, and I'll see you later."

In the car, Becky and I just looked at each other in amazement.

Becky was the first to speak. "Who would have believed Frank would make such an offer? And actually talk so much in the process?"

"Not me. But it sounds like a great idea. We'd be close enough to home for frequent visits, in both directions. And far enough away not to get on our children's nerves—and vice versa."

Becky's impulsiveness took over. "I'm sold. But we do need to at least talk to Mandy and Sonya about it. They don't have to know we've already made up our minds."

We walked in the center half an hour later to find most of our friends already there. After a lot of hugging, we gathered around the large table, and Lydia brought plates of cookies and reminded everyone where to find the coffee and soft drinks. Like they didn't all know. But I knew about caretakers—she wanted to make *sure* everyone knew.

I couldn't wait to hear news about Earl. "What did they find out about Earl's death?"

A knowing look passed around the table before Lydia answered. "Doc says he fell for some reason and when his head hit the pavement, it killed him. Just that simple."

"Simple, maybe, but it certainly messed up a couple of days for us. I'm glad it's over."

Becky had to get one more shot in at the sheriff. "That sheriff jumped the gun with us. If it hadn't been for Jake and Doug, we might be in the slammer. But we're not, so let's catch up with the rest of the news."

Jake asked the inevitable question. "Before we do that, what kind of trouble did you two get into while you were gone?"

Becky and I exchanged glances, both trying to decide just how much to tell them.

I decided that if we were going to live here, we might as well tell it all. "Well, I had a hard time keeping Becky out of a brawl in Tunica. Other than that we didn't get in much trouble."

All eyes turned to Becky. "It wasn't exactly a brawl. I just won a lot of money on a slot machine some other woman had just left. She was a little upset when she discovered my first quarter won me $1000"

"To put it mildly." I could hardly contain myself thinking about that old broad.

Becky kicked me under the table and changed the subject. "What's going on around here?"

Doug began a verbal countdown of the news. "Hank is ready to start college in January. Mamie is back in the cake making business. All of us are busy as community helpers—for pay, of course. And Lydia has started a tutoring service here at the center three days a week."

"Wow! You have been busy. How about Mike and Joan?" That young couple intrigued me.

"They're having a baby. They are so excited."

"Well, we'll have to be here for that event. Are they coming tonight for supper?"

Jake knew them best, so he took that question. "I'm sure they will. I'll call them in a minute to be sure. We're also going to invite Dr. Holloway and his wife. They are anxious to get to know the two of you. After all, I hear you may be moving here." He leaned forward and a big smile told everyone what he thought of the prospect.

"No secrets in Eddyville. We haven't decided yet. Have to talk to our kids first." I looked to see the expressions around the table. People looked hopeful but understanding.

It felt like home to be back with these dear people. And I was so glad that in this place, you could get everyone together with almost no notice. I had learned to love small town life.

I turned to Mamie. "Do you have desert ready for tonight?"

"It's thawing. Didn't know when you'd be here, so I made it and froze it ahead of time. I'll frost it in just a minute. It'll be ready to eat by the time you finish cooking. What are we having tonight?"

"How about spaghetti and meatballs and a salad and garlic toast?"

Jake jumped right on that. "Sounds great. Would you like me to go with you to the grocery?"

"That would be nice. We'd better get going. I'm thinking I won't be able to wait long to get into that cake of Mamie's."

I got up to leave and before I knew what was happening, Doug and Becky were walking out with us. Damn. No alone time today.

We were back at the center within the hour. Since I planned to do the tomato sauce and meatballs, Becky decided to stay out of the kitchen. She'd take her turn with the salad and bread.

Jake followed me into the kitchen where he gathered me into a hug in privacy. I was learning that he didn't much believe in public displays of emotion. We both put on an apron and got started. While I was putting together the sauce to simmer, he proceeded to start on the meatballs.

"You seem to know your way around a kitchen. Who taught you to make meatballs?"

There was a brief pause before he answered. "My wife and I used to have this once a week. It was one thing we had to make for ourselves, since no one around here ever serves it. She was a great cook and taught me how to do this. You don't mind me helping do you?"

"Why on earth would I mind?" I began browning the onions and peppers. "You sound like you still miss your wife."

"Her death almost killed me. We had been together for thirty years and eight months, and I didn't think I could go on without her. Somehow I did. That's what I love about this little town. We lift each other up when one of us thinks we can't go on. Eventually, I started coming here and then teaching line dancing at the Wild West and got on with life. I do still think about her though."

His honesty and his story touched me. I decided to respond in kind. "I know what you mean about not knowing if you could go on. When George died, I felt the same way. We had grown up together and thought we would grow old together. I still miss him. But I went on with life and seem to be in a good place right now. This trip has helped me in a lot of ways. I don't think I told you before, but things haven't been good with my daughter since her father died. During the course of this trip, we seem to have worked out some problems by phone. And Becky and I have had time to talk about the things seniors worry about. It has been a great thing for both of us." I turned to look out into the dining hall and smiled. "And we made some new friends and that is always welcome."

Becky and Doug replaced us in the kitchen while the meatballs were cooking in the oven. Jake showed me where the dishes and silverware were, and we began setting the table.

"How many places do we need to set?" I looked around at Lydia.

She came to help us. "I think there will be about twenty people including us. Everybody wants to see you and hear about your trip."

At 5 o'clock, people began coming in. Harold, Tubby, Joe, Hank, Mack. Helen, Mike, and Joan came in together. I congratulated Mike and Joan and then walked over to the one couple I didn't know. I introduced myself. "Hello. I didn't think there was anyone around here I didn't know. I'm Linda Burton."

He extended his hand. "Hi. I'm Dr. Holloway. And this is my wife Allison. We never had a chance to meet you before. Lydia invited us to join in the festivities tonight."

"I'm so glad you came." I looked around and couldn't see Becky anywhere. "Excuse me. I need to get back in the kitchen. Dinner is my treat for all you wonderful people." When I went in the kitchen expecting to find Becky there, it was empty. Good thing I came in because the meatballs were on the verge of burning. I pulled them out of the oven and stirred the tomato sauce before adding the meatballs. It was beginning to thicken and, by the time the sauce was just right, the meatballs would have absorbed some of the sauce. I started a pot of water for the spaghetti. Then I opened the door to the back deck to see if Becky and Doug were out there. They were definitely *there*. I retreated into the dining area.

Mamie was working on the cake with some freshly made frosting. It looked scrumptious. When she walked away, I was just reaching for a finger full of frosting when someone grabbed my arm. I looked up to see Jake's smiling face. "Caught in the act, Ms. Burton. Shame on you."

"Guilty as charged. Want to make it two swipes of icing?"

"Okay. But let's not mess up all Mamie's hard work decorating this. How about we swipe across the back—the part turned to the wall?"

"Ready?" Hand in air, I counted off and on three we each raked across the back of the cake and met in the middle. Then we licked the icing off our index fingers like overgrown children. We were enjoying our mischief when I heard water boiling over on the stove. I ran to the kitchen. Becky, though a bit disheveled, had done the same and had the top off the pot of water. I dropped the spaghetti in and she began dishing up the salad.

In another twenty minutes, we were all happily seated with a plate of spaghetti and all the trimmings in front of us. Lydia had made tea before we got there.

When dinner was over, I began clearing the table. Jake got up to help and just as I reached the kitchen door, I had a terrible pain in my arm. I barely recovered the plate that headed for the floor.

"Are you all right?" Jake hurried over to take the plate from me.

"I think so. Just a sharp pain. I haven't done much physical labor in a while. I guess I'm out of practice."

I continued clearing the table while Mamie cut cake for everyone. When she turned it around and saw the missing icing, she looked straight at me with a twinkle in her eye. "Was it good?"

"It was heavenly."

Seated with dessert plates full of chocolate cake, people talked ninety miles an hour. On my second luscious bite, I gasped for air and it felt like a truck fell on my chest. I must have looked awful, because all talking stopped and Dr. Holloway was at my side in ten seconds.

chapter

FOURTEEN

An hour later, I was sitting in the local hospital in one of those lovely little gowns. Dr. Holloway and Jake had hurried me there with Doug and Becky following behind. Dr. Holloway gave me a tiny pill to put under my tongue, as Jake drove like a bat out of hell. The pill stopped the pain, and I was breathing just fine again by the time we got to the emergency room.

"Okay. When can I get out of here? This gown is a little drafty." I could only imagine what I looked like sitting there with my bare legs showing out from under the overly small wrap-around garment. Actually, it didn't wrap around; it was more like a sneak-a-peek opportunity. That would not be very encouraging to Jake and any future possibilities.

Dr. Holloway laughed. "They don't exactly make those things with any substance. Linda, you had an angina attack. I'm not as concerned since the medication took care of it, and your EKG looks fine. But when you get home, you need to get your doctor to see whether you have blockage or any other heart problem. Can I count on you doing that?"

"I guess. But when can I leave here? I wanted to go dancing after supper."

"You won't be going dancing. If I have to check you in here, I will. Now will you get those tests at home, or should I schedule them here?" Dr. Holloway locked his eyes on mine.

"Well, just do it here. Let me call my daughter first."

"Fine. You call your daughter, and I'll get our cardiologist to come in and decide which tests need to be done." He turned and left before I could change my mind.

I punched in Mandy's number while my friends went for a cup of coffee. Mandy answered on the third ring. "Mom. How are things?"

"Well, okay. I had a bit of a heart incident at supper and wanted to let you know that before they start poking and prodding me."

Her voice rose two octaves. "What kind of heart incident? Are you all right?"

"Yes, I'm fine. Just stay calm. The doctor was at the senior center when it happened, and he and Jake rushed me to the hospital here. By the time I got here, I was fine. Dr. Holloway gave me a nitroglycerin tablet to put under my tongue, and it took care of the problem. He wants to be sure there is no blockage. The cardiologist will decide what test to do. But I am fine."

"Well, what kind of hospital and doctors do they have in such a small town? I think you should come home and do this stuff."

"They have a good regional hospital and it's connected to the medical school in St. Louis. If they find anything to worry about, I'll come home and finish there with Dr. Blake. Now don't worry. I'll call you when the tests are finished."

"Don't bother. I'll be on my way there. I can be there in about four hours."

"Mandy, that is so sweet of you. If you'll feel better to do that, I'll be glad to see you. But if you want to wait and see what they find, that's okay too."

"No. I'm coming. I'll take the kids over to Sonya's. I'll get her to drive and that way, I can drive you home in your car and she can bring Becky back in her car. I'll see you in four or five hours. What's your doctor's name?"

"Dr. Holloway. Do you want him to call you when he comes back to my room?"

" Yes. Give him my cell number. I'll keep it on. I'll see you soon, and I love you, Mom. I love you a lot."

"Me too, sweetie. With all my heart—even if it turns out to be a diseased heart."

I was just putting the phone in my purse when Dr. Holloway entered the room. "I've got someone coming to get you. The cardiologist decided on a CT scan. It won't take long, but you'll have to stay here until the cardiologist can look at it."

"That's fine. My daughter wants to talk to you. Here's her cell number. She said she would leave it on."

"How about I wait until the CT scan is finished and then I'll be able to tell her more."

"That's a good idea. She'll be on her way here. This has unnerved her, I think."

"First time you've had a serious health issue?"

"Yes. And her father died very suddenly many years ago, and I imagine that's playing over in her mind right now."

"I'll reassure her. Even if we find something on the scan, you didn't have a heart attack, and that probably means we have time to work on anything that is amiss. I have a daughter myself—I'll make her feel better."

Just at that moment, they came to take me down to x-ray. I was feeling much better physically and reassured about Dr. Holloway talking with Mandy.

When I came rolling down the hall an hour later, the waiting room was full of people I knew. They were huddled together comparing notes on medical emergencies I'm sure. Nevertheless, they cared enough to be here, and that made me feel good. Lydia spotted me and came over to talk, as we continued down the hall. "Well, you sure can make a dramatic exit. How're you feeling?"

"I'm fine now. I didn't have a heart attack, and I'll probably be out of here in another couple of hours. Thanks for coming to check on me. I tried to get the doctor to let me go dancing tonight but he said no."

"Linda, behave yourself. I saved half of Mamie's cake for you. That should make you feel better." Lydia had my number, even though we'd only known each other a short time.

"All right. I'll be out of here for sure tonight. I'll take that cake with me to Frank's Place."

I was back in my room and trying to think of a way to hike my butt into the bed without total exposure. I had a flashback to that men's locker room on the first day of our trip. It was not a pretty picture.

I maneuvered myself onto the bed before the others came in. Becky had filled them in, and they no longer looked as scared as they'd been an hour earlier.

"When can you leave?" Becky still looked a little worried, but then she knew I probably would not follow the rules.

"I'm not sure. Mandy and Sonya are driving down here. I couldn't talk them out of it. Sonya is driving so Mandy can drive me home, and you and Sonya can have some private time to talk on the way home in her car."

"Well, we made quite an exit from home and looks like we'll make an equally dramatic re-entrance. They may never let us leave home again."

I raised my eyebrows. "Oh, yes they will. I'd say around about Thanksgiving time."

Becky's face broke into a grin. "Indeed. Thanksgiving weekend sounds right to me."

I was home by nightfall the next day, having been given a more or less clean bill of health. No explanation for the angina but lots of instructions for preventing it from happening again. Exercise, healthy food, less stress, and some rest for the next month. I had it all figured out. Sex is good exercise and a great stress reliever. Once we moved to Eddyville, I might have those two covered with Jake. Healthy food—maybe. I would rest from now until we moved to Eddyville.

chapter

FIFTEEN

I loved October. It was the month George and I married and the month Mandy was born. But this October was the best of all. Mandy had come home emotionally. It was hard to remember how things had been before. She came every day after work for two weeks, she brought me food and drink, and she did not ask anything of me. We laughed and joked like we used to, and we enjoyed each other's company for the first time in a long while. Life was good.

My rehab helped me to get stronger every day and to have more energy. I thought I had lots of energy before, but I must have been running on adrenaline and grit. Now I felt truly good and began to experience the pleasure of being fit again. Becky often joined me on my morning walk, and we always reviewed our adventure and talked about Jake and Doug, who called every few days. Who would have thought we would find "boy friends" at this point in our lives? I was not sure where that was going but I planned to enjoy it.

Today I was expecting Becky to join me for my daily walk. October was about over, and I didn't want to miss a single day of being outdoors.

We had plenty to talk about this morning. Doug and Jake would be here for the weekend and we needed to plan. I was sure where Doug would stay, but I had no clue where Jake would sleep.

When the doorbell rang, I grabbed my keys off the counter and went out ready to walk.

Becky asked her daily question. "How are you feeling this morning?"

"I feel great. And we need to plan our weekend while we walk."

"Well, let's get started. When did Jake say they would get here?"

"He thought they would be here about 8 Friday night. So the first question is where will they stay?"

"Well, I know where Doug is staying." The way her eyes lit up made me happy.

"I'm not sure where Jake will stay. I have extra bedrooms, of course, but how will it look to the neighbors, as my mother used to say." I guess none of us gets too far from our upbringing.

"Who cares? If they even notice, they'll just be envious. How many old biddies our age have sleepovers with men?" Becky did a middle-aged version of a giggle.

"Believe me, they will notice. When was the last time we did anything the whole town didn't know about?" I turned toward Becky with eyes widening.

"Well, that's true. But what other choices do you have? Mandy doesn't have room and frankly, I don't want any extra people at my house. Doug and I might get a little rambunctious." She looked at me out of the corner of her eyes, while watching the rutted path we had taken.

"I expect you will. And you know what, I'm happy for you. We've both been alone too long, and that's one of the best lessons of our trip. Having friends to go places with and do things with is not the same as having someone special. "

"So you still think Jake is special? I wasn't sure and didn't want to do my usual barging right in to ask." She looked at me with a half smile.

"Lord, Becky. Have you learned to be diplomatic? Amazing. To answer your question, I thought I was too old to get that tingle again, but I'm not. We're a long way from getting rambunctious, as you put it, but he is definitely someone different from my escorts around here."

"So where is he going to stay?"

"I don't know. I hate for him to drive all this way and stay in a motel, but I don't think I'm ready for him to stay at my house, even in the extra bedroom."

"Could Mandy send the kids to your house and have him stay there?"

"Hey, that's a great idea. I want the two of them to get to know each other, and I always enjoy time with the grandkids. I'll ask her about that today. There's plenty of time for her to get a room ready for him. Maybe I'll lend her Maggie, to clean the house and make up a guest room. Do you think she would be offended by that?" I still tiptoed around our new relationship.

"A year ago she would have taken your offer and never said thank you. Now she might want to do it herself. Why don't you just run the idea by her? Does she know the guys are coming for the weekend?"

"I told her last night when we talked. You know, we talk every night, and it warms my heart every time the phone rings."

Becky patted my arm. "I know it does. It almost warms my cold, old heart too."

"There is hope for all of us if your cold, old heart is thawing!" It was good to be back to our usual jabbing at each other. There for a week or two after the heart incident we lost that.

When we were back at my front door, I asked, "Want to come in for breakfast?" It was a tentative question at best. Becky was not fond of my healthy breakfast routine.

"If you can come up with something totally unhealthy for me. We need to get our plans set, and then I have to go home and clean."

I put my healthy breakfast together and put two doughnuts out for Becky, while we continued to plan. "I really think Jake staying at Mandy's is a good idea except for one thing. I won't have any time alone with Jake. "

"Isn't that your point?

"No. I'm just not ready to sleep with him yet. But I definitely want some time to ourselves."

"Have you talked to him about this? Maybe he already has plans to stay in a motel."

"I don't know. I was so excited to hear he was coming for a visit, I didn't even ask.

"Why don't you just wait and play it by ear? There will always be a room available at the Best Western—we don't get many tourists through here."

"Good idea. Thank goodness you have a pragmatic side as well as a wild streak."

She stopped chewing and thought a minute. "Yeah, I do. And a good thing, since you're such a worry wart."

When we finished eating, Becky started out the door. She turned to hand out one more piece of advice. "Don't pass up this opportunity out of fear, Linda. It's okay to enjoy your life—even a sex life. George would not want you to be alone forever."

"I know. But I'm afraid. Sixty-something is very different from forty-something. I'll just see how it goes."

"Linda! Think back to that locker room you walked into. He'll be sagging, too. Just be sure the lights are off."

"Oh, hush. Go home and clean your house."

I walked back into the house thinking about Jake, the weekend, and Becky's advice. I had no idea how the weekend would go but I knew it would be a welcome visit.

Over the next few days, we decided to have the guys come to my house first, and then Becky and Doug could leave from there. That wouldn't take long, I suspected. Of course, that meant Jake would be at my house with no transportation.

At exactly eight o'clock Friday night, the doorbell rang. Becky and I did the age-old female thing—smoothed our hair and glanced in the mirror in the hall. Some things don't change with age.

I opened the door to some very happy looking guests. Walking into the hallway, I noticed Jake had his overnight bag. He set it by the antique tall clock and I pretended not to notice.

In the living room, I poured wine before we gathered in front of my first fire of the season. It wasn't cool enough for a fire but, in my mind, a fire was always part of welcoming very wanted guests after the first of September. I'm sure there must have been a lesson there somewhere.

"How was your drive?" I asked.

"It was okay. I might have gone to sleep if I hadn't had Jake to talk to though. I'm not used to driving this far this close to bed time." Doug wanted to steer this conversation too, but not into my definition of safe territory.

Becky jumped in at this point. "Tell us all about Eddyville. How is Tubby? And Lydia?"

"Everybody says hello. Tubby is still bringing food to the center and Lydia is still keeping everything organized."

"And how about the Wild West Saloon? Has Hank gone off to college?" I was proud of our part in that.

Doug and Becky were snuggled together on the sofa having a private conversation by now. Jake sat across from me in the other leather chair by the fireplace. "Yes. He comes home every weekend, but he's really enjoying not having to work on weekends. He hopes to finish in three years if he goes to summer school. Then he's coming back to Eddyville, of course."

"He loves that place. I wonder what he will do when he comes back to live."

"He was serious about running for sheriff. That will be a good thing. How are you?"

"I'm just great. I haven't felt better in years. That heart episode may have been the best thing that ever happened to me."

Jake was quiet for a minute. "You seem different. I'm not sure exactly how."

"I think I am different. Sometimes I don't like that. Other times it seems inevitable."

"What do you mean?"

"Oh, I seem to be less..." I searched for just the right word. "... frivolous. I am not always going for the laugh. I'm not sure I like that change, frankly."

"Maybe it will shift again in time. Without the need for another angina attack, I hope."

"Me too. One of those is quite enough."

Just then, Doug and Becky got up and announced that they were going to adjourn to Becky's house.

"You two behave. We'll see you for breakfast in the morning."

"Well—I'll pay attention to half of that." Becky gave me a quick hug, and they were out the door.

Now the awkward time began. I still was not entirely sure what to do—or not do.

Just to be on the safe side, I had made a reservation for Jake at the Best Western.

Only for one night.

We walked back to our chairs in front of the fire. I could hear the tall clock chiming in the hallway. It all felt so comfortable and comforting.

Jake spoke first. "I have a reservation at the Best Western. Let's just catch up with the news and then you can drive me over there."

I managed to keep a straight face. "Actually, you have two rooms reserved. I reserved one for you, too." We burst out laughing and the tension eased.

"I'm glad we are in agreement."

"Me, too."

"Back to the news. How is Mandy? Will I get to meet her this weekend?"

"She is wonderful. And yes, everybody is coming for dinner tomorrow night. You and Doug will have your fill of family by the time you leave here."

"I doubt that. Remember, the two of us don't have any family around. It will be a treat for us. Can I help you get dinner ready tomorrow?"

"I was hoping you would say that. It's been a while since I cooked for..." I counted on my fingers, "eleven people."

"Then maybe I'd better get going. I'm tired from the drive, and we'll need lots of energy tomorrow." He got up, picked up his luggage as he went through the hall, and we were off to the Best Western. Before my heart attack, I would have made some smart-assed remark about this whole situation, but not now. Which was the real me? I no longer knew, and I found that unsettling.

chapter

SIXTEEN

After the weekend visit, we decided it was time to give Frank an answer and tell our girls about this new venture. Becky was coming this morning to talk about that. I heard her come in the front door. Knock three times and open the door—that was our philosophy.

"Hey. How's it going? And I hope to God you bought me some doughnuts." She dropped her sweater on the nearest chair and sat at the kitchen table.

"Yes. You have doughnuts. I'll just sprinkle a little granola over them for good measure." I stood poised with a handful of the dreaded stuff.

"Do it and die. How do you eat that? It's like chewing on shingles."

With our divergent breakfasts in front of us, we began to think aloud. Me first. "We need to give Frank an answer, and then we need to decide when to tell the kids."

"Let's call Frank while I'm here. Then we can plan for telling the kids and grandkids. Think they will miss us?"

"Most days. Not all days. Matt and Melinda are really enjoying more time with their Mom and less time with me. It's more like a real family for them. How about Sonya?"

"She's calmed down a lot about my health, and I think she's impressed with my ability to take care of myself without her help. Not to mention taking care of you."

"Ha! The only taking care of me you did was when you held my legs while I was hanging out that window. And you kept threatening to let go. That's probably why I had an angina attack."

"A week later—I don't think so. Hurry up and finish that yogurt and shingles, and let's call Frank."

Becky began to dial while I put the few dishes in the sink. Even though we could hardly contain our excitement, I motioned for her to stop dialing.

"What's your problem?" she asked with obvious irritation, as she hung up the phone.

"Do you think maybe we ought to give this a little more thought? We've lived here forever. Are you sure we're ready to leave and live in a new place?"

It was quiet for a minute while Becky looked down at her hands and licked off the doughnut glaze. "Maybe we should." She looked up, "I find myself driving around town and tearing up when I see places with special memories. I know it's silly, but I've lived and loved in this town a long time."

"I know. I do the same thing. I even tear up when I see a place that reminds me of a bad memory. What the hell is wrong with us?"

"We seem to have done a lot of crying in the last month. Maybe we're getting senile. You know how batty, old people cry all the time."

"And exactly how many batty, old people do you know, Becky?"

"Just you." She licked the last of the doughnut glaze off her finger and stepped back to avoid my fake slap.

"I think we need to go for a walk and talk about this some more. I love Eddyville. I may even love Jake. And I'd love to have a new career. However, I'm not so sure I want all that enough to leave home and family. Let's talk about it some more so we'll be sure what we want to do."

"You're repeating yourself, Linda." She stuck her arm in her sweater as she talked. "But unfortunately, I think you may be right."

"Okay. Where shall we walk this morning?"

"Let's just walk around the neighborhood."

I pulled on a sweatshirt to ward off the autumn chill. The weather was perfect for walking. Bright sunny day, moderate temperatures with a cool breeze, and that clear blue sky that made me love autumn.

"Look at that sky, Becky. Not a cloud in it."

"Yeah. Remember when we would take Mandy and Sonya out in their strollers? They used to watch the clouds and ask 'what dat?' until I thought I would scream."

"I remember. Isn't it funny how we miss things that used to irritate the hell out of us? Now I remember those times with such a warm spot in my heart. God, I can't believe how sentimental I'm getting." I paused before continuing. "Maybe the tears are really about not wanting to leave here. I usually just make my decisions and move on, but this one is pulling me in both directions."

"Do you think maybe we see it as our last important or fun decision?"

"I hope not. We're not that old."

"I know. I'm just grasping for answers to my sudden over-sentimentality."

We walked on past the newer homes in the area. Our houses were built many years ago, but the area had continued to develop and the newer houses had character too—siding, dormers, porches. It still felt like a real neighborhood. That was one of those rare flashes of insight. "You know what I think is making me hesitate? A little unexpected snobbery. Do I really want to go from living in a nice neighborhood in the town where my friends and family are to living in an apartment in a motel?"

"Geeze, when you put it that way, I'm not so sure I do either." We walked in silence for another block before Becky continued. "But we'll be running that motel and having fun with Doug and Jake. Maybe more than fun. And we have friends there."

"Damn. This is going to be one of those decisions where the pros and cons come out even. I hate those decisions." I walked with my head down thinking. "Who can we ask to help us think through this? Not the children 'cause then they would feel responsible if something went badly. And I'm not paying a shrink to help us. How about Elizabeth? She mentioned having lunch together, and she's a smart cookie. In fact, I think she has a background in psychology. Lord knows, we could use that. "

"That's a great idea. Anybody who loves slot machines can't be bad. Let's go home, call her, and invite her to lunch next week. I'll bet she can help us." Becky's gait changed, and my shoulders straightened at the thought of getting help with this decision. By next week, we could call Frank and give him an answer. I hoped.

The phone rang later in the day, and the caller ID showed Elizabeth's name.

"Hello there. How nice to hear from you. I was going to call you today. We need to plan that lunch we talked about in Tunica."

"I agree. That's why I'm calling. Could you and Becky come to my house for lunch tomorrow?"

"Hey, that sounds wonderful. I'll call Becky and if you don't hear differently, we'll count on that. What time should we come?"

"How about coming around 10:30 and we can talk and catch up with each other before lunch?"

"Great. We'll see you then—and if Becky can't come, I'll call you right back."

"Okay. I'm looking forward to seeing the two of you again."

I dialed Becky's number and she was as happy as I was to go to lunch and see Elizabeth again.

At 10:35 the next day, we rang the bell at Elizabeth's house. It was a Tudor style home in the best part of town. I could hardly wait to see the inside, especially that room with the four hundred dollar a yard fabric.

The door opened, and Elizabeth greeted us with a hug. "It's great to see you again. And this time I don't even have to rescue you."

Stepping inside we found exactly what I would have expected— an entryway with the living room on the left and the dining room on the right and all impeccably decorated.

"Thanks for inviting us for lunch. I don't know where the time has gone since our little Tunica adventure." I parked myself in the overstuffed wing chair and felt right at home. Elizabeth could probably make the King of England feel at home.

Becky spoke up. "And I want you to know, I have not had any more unpleasant encounters to hide from."

There was wine and a tray of appetizers on the coffee table. I helped myself and asked what was going on in her world.

"Oh, just the usual. Teenage daughters take a lot of energy and a lot of driving around. I am beginning to understand why people buy their children cars so early."

"Lord, I remember that rat race. I'm glad to be past it."

Becky couldn't wait to tell her our offer in Eddyville. "Well, we have some news. Frank has asked us to move to Eddyville and help him run his motel. We're thinking about doing that."

Her eyes widened. "You're kidding."

"We can't decide. At first we were sure we would, but now we both find ourselves having a hard time thinking about leaving here." I hoped this would elicit some comment from Elizabeth.

"You've lived here your whole adult life, haven't you? I would think that would make it hard to leave."

Becky stuck her thumb in my direction and said, "Ole teary eyes there keeps getting all misty about the whole thing."

"Like you don't? The truth is we're both having second thoughts."

Elizabeth busied herself with the food and napkins on the coffee table. "Gosh, I'd hate for you to go. We're just really getting acquainted, and I was depending on you going to Vegas with me sometime."

"Ohh. Wouldn't that be fun? I could play some big time slot machines there."

"Well, nothing says we couldn't still do that. Eddyville is not that far away. Have you ever been there, Elizabeth?" I inquired.

"Not really. But hearing you all talk about it has been fun. And watching your eyes light up when you talk about Jake and Doug is especially nice."

Just then, the timer went off in the kitchen, and we were left on our own in the living room.

"She's so nice. When should we ask her advice about this move?"

Becky thought before answering. "Let's wait until after lunch. Wouldn't want her to think we only came to get advice."

"You're right. Maybe when we're back in here just chatting."

Lunch was delicious, and we made quick work of it. Bringing our wine back into the living room, I opened the conversation about our move. "What do you think we should do about Frank's offer?"

"I don't know. How are the two of you feeling about leaving home?"

Becky answered first. "I'm excited about a new adventure, but I keep tearing up all over town. I don't know what's wrong with me."

"Maybe nothing is wrong with you. Maybe you're just having a hard time seeing yourself living somewhere else. After all, you've been here your whole life. Leaving must be hard."

I spoke up next. "I'm embarrassed to admit this, but I keep thinking about moving from a nice house and a nice neighborhood into living quarters in a motel. I'm sorry, but that's a bit of a comedown."

Elizabeth was quiet before she answered. "I agree. You need to think about the pride issue in doing that. Don't you think it's important to be proud of where you live?"

"I do. Yet that makes me feel like such a snob. I never thought of myself that way."

"Is it snobbery or not wanting to look like you've been a failure in life?"

"How did you get so wise in so few years? I think you have hit on exactly what it is. But where am I going to find a Jake in Millerton?"

Becky had been quiet during this exchange, and what she said next really surprised me. "I think our real choice is whether to stay put where we know we are happy or go start a new adventure which might not be as happy as we first thought."

Elizabeth let silence fill the room. After a bit, she responded. "I think that is exactly the choice, and it's not an easy one. All I can say is don't just think it through—feel it through as well. You seem to feel strongly about both sides of this decision. Those are the hardest decisions to make. I don't envy your task."

We moved on to other topics and in another hour, we gathered our things and left for home and some soul searching. One thing I knew—we had to tell the girls before we went any further.

We decided to talk to our daughters separately, but on the same night. No chance of being ganged up on and no chance for them to plot their strategy together, if they objected.

On a Wednesday night, we each invited our children to come for dinner. This was not unusual, and I hoped the evening discussion would not be too unusual. I knew if Mandy was truly against this idea or if it appeared to hurt her feelings, I would not go through with it. Becky had no reservations along those lines.

After dinner that night, Mandy and the children and I sat in the family room as we now did after any family dinner. When the conversation lagged, I took a deep breath and jumped in.

"Mandy, you know Becky and I made a lot of friends in Eddyville. We really like that little town. What did you think of it?"

"The people seemed wonderful when you were sick, and the town's kind of cute. And I love Jake and Doug. I wouldn't want to live there, but it has a certain charm to it."

"Funny you should say that. Becky and I have decided we might like to live there."

"You're kidding! Where would you live?"

"Frank—the man that runs the motel we stayed in—asked us if we would help him run the place in exchange for private living quarters. We'll probably tell him okay, but if you think it's a bad idea, I won't go. I care what you think."

Even the children were rendered speechless by that news. After a few seconds, Mandy answered. "I think it's a good idea. I know you've been bored here, and I know you did too much for me for a long time. I think it's time for you to do what you want to do."

I almost leapt out of my chair in my haste to give her a hug. Patting her on the back, I said, "Oh, honey. Thank you. I've thought a lot about this. I'm excited about it, but if it doesn't work out the way we think,

I'll still have this house, and Frank can just turn our living quarters back into rooms to rent. Thank you."

"We can visit you, and you can come home for long visits. Who knows—maybe it will be a great place to spend holidays together. More festive than always being here. Oh, I don't mean I don't like it here, but it's kind of hard to create a celebration with such a small family. There we'll have lots of new family."

"Mandy, you are so dear. Let me run another idea by you. Would you and Matt and Melinda like to live here?"

At this point Matt and Melinda chimed in. "Can we Mom? Oh, can we?"

"I'll think about that. And kids, you need to think about it, too. All your friends are in our neighborhood. I don't know if this is in the same school district or not. Let me get back to you about that."

"No hurry. I am not going to sell the house regardless. I'll be coming home often, and eventually we'll probably move back here—when we are really old."

Mandy laughed aloud. "I don't care how many years you live, you will never be really old. But I am glad that you plan to move back eventually. That's nice."

"We haven't totally decided to do this. But I wanted to know how you felt about it before we decide."

"I appreciate that, and I'll support you either way."

We ended the night on such a positive note that I couldn't begin to put my feelings into words. I hoped it was going as well for Becky. I promised her I would not call until tomorrow. Even Becky occasionally needed her privacy.

At 7 o'clock the next morning, I sat in the family room with a cup of coffee, waiting for Becky to call. If she didn't call by eight, I would call her. The phone rang at 7:15.

"How did it go?" I held my breath waiting for the answer.

"Pretty good. They were shocked at first but by the time they left, Sonya was okay with it. And once they had time to think, they weren't even surprised. They know what fun we had there and how much we like Doug and Jake. How did it go there?"

"Great. Mandy was totally for the idea and understood why I wanted to move. She and I have come a long way. Mandy really was happy for me."

"Then we need to make a final decision and get busy packing what we're taking. Do you think Doug and Jake could come over and haul the stuff to Eddyville?" My little medical crisis and this new venture had turned Becky into a planner. Thank God. Her spontaneous self could be unnerving—not to mention exhausting. I'd enjoy this new Becky, while it lasted.

"I'll bet they could get a truck and extra muscle power. And Ralph can help load, too. Right now, I have a doctor's appointment. He may prove to be more of a problem than Mandy."

"Well, work that female magic on him, like you did on Frank when we first checked in at his place. I'll talk to you this afternoon."

chapter

SEVENTEEN

Sitting in the den alone that night, I focused my mind on the pros and cons of moving to Eddyville. The pro list began with being near Jake. It continued with activities and people I enjoyed, new beginnings of all sorts, an easy job, and being appreciated for my talents. The con list began with being away from Mandy and the grandchildren, leaving a renewed relationship with Mandy, moving to less pleasant surroundings, leaving my home of many years, the distance when something was wrong with me or with Mandy and her family, and I finally added fear of the unknown. I knew I liked the people at Eddyville, and they liked me, and I knew I more than liked Jake, but where that might lead was scary. Did I want to begin a real relationship? Did I want to risk moving there only to find that Jake or I did not want that as much as we thought? Sexual desire and sassy sexual comments were quite different from stripping to the skin after age sixty. Maybe I should just stay put and buy myself a good vibrator.

I wondered what thoughts were going through Becky's head. We had agreed to give this decision more serious thought tonight and talk about it tomorrow. I got up and started for the phone to invite Becky to breakfast, but the phone rang before I got to it.

I checked the caller ID and saw that it was a call from Eddyville. I didn't recognize the number.

"Hello."

"Linda, this is Lydia. I thought you'd like to know that Jake has been in a terrible accident. He's in the same hospital you were in, and they are not sure he will make it."

"Oh, my God. Becky and I will be there as soon as we can get there. Are you at the hospital?"

"No. I just got home. But Doug was going to stay all night with him. He doesn't have any family around you know."

"I know. I'll call Becky, and we will get on the road as soon as possible. Thanks for calling me, Lydia."

"Oh, I knew you'd want to know. I'll call Frank and tell him to have two rooms ready for you all. I'll see you tomorrow."

"Thanks. I'll be there soon and if you talk to Doug, tell him that."

"I will. Be careful. You can't help Jake if you have an accident yourself, you know."

"I will. See you soon, Lydia."

The moment I could get a dial tone, I called Becky. "Becky, we have to go to that hospital near Eddyville. Jake was injured in an accident, and they're not sure he'll make it."

"Oh, God. I'll be ready in half an hour. Just pack the necessities, and let's get on the road. Was Doug with him?"

"He's at the hospital with him, but he wasn't in the accident. Thank God he is staying with him tonight."

After throwing a change of clothes and all my medications in a bag, I called Mandy to tell her the news. She promised to take care of everything at home, and I promised to call her when we got there.

Becky walked across the street with an overnight bag half an hour later, and we were on our way.

When we arrived at the hospital a few hours later, I saw Doug coming out of Jake's room. "How is he doing?"

"He's holding his own. I know he'll be glad to see you."

"What is his worst injury?"

Doug looked thoughtful for a moment. "Well, he ruptured his spleen and broke his leg. He lost a lot of blood too and all together it's dangerous."

"Will he need a lot of rehab time?"

"We hope so." I guessed that was Doug's way of reminding me that he was in danger.

I started for the door of his room, and Doug put his hand on my shoulder. "He looks pretty awful, and he's taking a lot of pain medication. Don't expect too much."

I steeled myself to put on a good act, as I had done so many times with Mandy. Pushing the door open, I managed not to gasp when I saw him. He looked awful and so lifeless. I took a deep breath and walked to the side of his bed.

"Don't you dare die on me, Jake. Not just as we are getting so close. Don't you dare do that to me."

He moved his arm and slowly opened one eye. "Well. When did you get here?"

"About five minutes ago. How are you?"

"About like I look, I think. I'm just beginning to be sort of awake."

"You have about scared me to death. What happened?' I straightened the covers as I talked.

"I'm not sure. They said I was out for about an hour."

I took his hand that didn't have an IV in it and looked straight into his eyes. "Well, you remember this. I am not going home without you. You can stay at my house and see my doctor and physical therapist for your rehab. But I am not leaving here until you do, and you are going home with me."

The beginning of a smile tugged at one corner of his mouth. "Yes, ma'am. I'm yours for the taking."

"Hmmm. That sounds interesting. More than interesting." I was quiet for a minute. Then I looked at his leg in traction and said, "I'm trying to figure out exactly how that might work."

His speech began to slur, but I thought I heard him say, "We'll find a way," just before he dropped off to sleep again.

I kissed his forehead and went out to find someone who could tell me more about his condition. Doug and Becky were in deep conversation, but I barged right in. "Who is his doctor, Doug?"

"Doc Holloway. He also called in a surgeon and an orthopedic guy. I guess Dr. Holloway would be the best person for you to talk to."

"Well, I'm staying here until he can leave, and then I'm taking him home with me. And don't either of you say a word."

Becky pulled me down in a chair beside her. "I think that is exactly what should be done. He can't go home alone." She turned to look at Doug. "And you can come and visit whenever you like and stay at my place."

"Sounds like a good plan. But it will be a while, and the next twenty-four hours will be the make or break period. I thought we were going to lose him, and they're still not sure he'll be okay."

"He'll be okay. I told him he was forbidden to die. Not just when we found each other."

Doug and Becky exchanged wide-eyed looks of amazement.

"Well, don't act like you're surprised. We're in love—we just haven't had the courage to say it out loud yet."

Just then, I saw Doc Holloway walking down the hall. I went to meet him halfway, hoping he would talk to me even if I wasn't family—yet.

A week later, I drove into my driveway with Jake in the passenger seat, which was pushed back and reclined to accommodate the cast on his leg. Not only had he survived, he was recovering at a remarkable rate. I promised Doc Holloway I would take him to my doctor the next day.

Jake began to open the door before I yelled at him. "You wait right there until I can get around there and help you. I don't want you falling in my driveway and then suing me."

"Yes, Ma'am. Though I may sue you for bossiness."

As I helped him get steady on his feet, Doug and Becky drove into the driveway behind us. Doug hopped out and quickly took over the steadying chores, and Becky and I walked ahead to unlock my back door.

"What *will* the neighbors think?" Becky couldn't stop goading me about this arrangement. Like she and Doug hadn't been sharing a bed for weeks.

"You know what? When you compare losing Jake to that, I don't give a rat's ass what they think."

"Wow. To quote a saying of the sixties, you've come a long way baby. Bravo."

"Yeah. Well you didn't have as far to go, I guess."

Mandy had cleaned the house and made up the bed in the guest room, so I walked Jake in there. I was only partially right in thinking he was tired. When I bent to pull the covers up over him, he grabbed me and pulled me down on the bed with more strength that I would have imagined. Then he proceeded to give me a warm, unexpected, and welcome kiss. Leaving the room, I thought, "Hmmm. Maybe we'll figure a way around that broken leg."

chapter

EIGHTEEN

In a few weeks, Jake was ready to go home. Doug drove in on Friday night, and they planned to go back to Eddyville on Saturday. I was busy preparing breakfast for all of us that Saturday morning.

Jake walked into the kitchen and sat at the kitchen table. "I could settle in here for a long time. Waking up to the smell of breakfast cooking feels good. I've missed all this."

"I know what you mean. I've missed having a reason to get up and make breakfast. I thought I was fine the way things were, but I think I was lonely."

"Yeah. Me. too. It's been a pleasant surprise to realize I don't have to stay that way."

"Oh. Planning to extend your visit?" I turned with both fear and hope.

"Not unless I'm invited to." He looked over with that impish half smile.

"I'll have to take that under consideration. After all, I'll be moving to Eddyville soon, I think. Becky and I have to finish talking about that and call Frank. He's been patient 'cause he knows you're here, but he deserves an answer from us."

"What do you think you'll do?"

"We have a bit of a dilemma. Neither of us wants to leave our home in Millerton, but we really would enjoy a new beginning in Eddyville. That's what we have to work out."

Jake was quiet for a few minutes, watching me cook and enjoying his first cup of coffee. He raised his head with a question mark on his face. "We could get married I guess and live in my house."

I almost dropped the bowl of hash browns I was mixing into a casserole. "What? Did you suggest we get married?" With a better grip on the mixing bowl, I turned to look at him.

"Sort of." He kept his face clear of expression.

"How do you 'sort of' ask someone to marry you? Geeze. That's romantic."

"I know. I shouldn't have said it. It's a logical thought, but I guess I'm not quite there." He didn't look me in the eye, and that was revealing.

"Jake, let me be honest. I love you, and I love the idea of us. But I'm not there either. I may never be. But I certainly enjoy what we have shared the last few weeks. More than enjoyed it. We even managed to find a way to work—or play—around that cast on your leg. That's pretty good for two old geezers."

"Who are you calling an old geezer? Maybe you, but not me."

"Really? Well, if memory serves me correctly, you are a few years older than me."

"Okay, you're right. I was hoping you forgot that little fact. Let's just enjoy what we have for now—maybe forever. I'm not sure it could be improved on."

I released an audible sigh of relief. I'd been alone a long time, and I wasn't anxious to change that.

Just then, I heard the familiar three knocks that announced Becky's arrival. "Hey," I called, "come on in the kitchen. I'm almost finished, and we can have some coffee in here while everything cooks."

When we had our coffee and were settled at the table, I brought up the idea of what to tell Frank. "We have to give Frank an answer. Becky, what are you thinking is the solution to our dilemma?"

"I'm hoping we can figure out a way to continue life here and start life there. Do you think we could get things up and running and then alternate weeks here and weeks there?"

"Hmm. That has possibilities. How long would it take you to do the decorating? I can set up a process for a continental breakfast fairly quickly, I think."

"If we work together, I think I could have the place decorated in a month. Maybe then, we could begin alternating weeks there. Do you think Frank would go for that?"

Jake chimed in at this point. "I suspect Frank might like that. He's been alone a long time, and too many people around may not be as welcome as he thinks."

I looked at Doug. "What do you think, Doug?"

"Well, if he is anything like me, it would be hard to give up all of my alone time. I'm enjoying sharing time with you, Becky, but I wouldn't be ready to give up all my time alone." I was happy to see that did not upset Becky. I suspected they had talked about this already. I guess we were as liberated as we thought. Neither of us just dying to get married. Ah, children of the sixties.

"Let's call and run this by Frank after breakfast. Any other ideas to run by him?"

What Mandy had said about Christmas celebrations made me have what I thought was a great idea, but I wanted to listen to the others first. No one spoke up, so I jumped in. "I was thinking it would be great fun to have a Christmas Day community celebration at Frank's Place. There are lots of people there who live alone, and others aren't able to do the whole Christmas dinner thing any more."

The other three reacted in a positive way to this. Becky was the most enthusiastic. "I love that idea. We could invite our children and grandchildren, and they could get to know all our friends there. We could decorate the tree, have a pitch-in dinner, and then sing carols and take home leftovers."

The timer on the oven buzzed at that moment, so conversation stopped while I got everything out of the oven and ready to serve. The four of us were comfortable enough to serve our plates from the stovetop.

Seated at the table, with plates of food and glasses of orange juice, conversation picked up where we left it and by the end of the meal, Christmas was planned and ready to present to Frank.

While Jake and Doug cleaned the kitchen, which was definitely a part of sharing my life that I liked, Becky took the phone into the living room to call Frank.

He answered on the third ring. "Hello."

"Hey, Frank. Becky here. How you doing?'

"Fine. Just wondering when I'd hear from you two."

"Here we are—about ready to report for duty, if that offer is still good."

"Yep. I think we can help each other."

"We'd like to run a couple of ideas by you before we move. How would you feel about us coming and getting everything decorated and the continental breakfast process set up and maybe even do a little advertising for you, then having us alternate weeks there? We both want to keep our houses here and stay in touch with our family and friends, but we want to be there too. We're hoping this compromise might be just the answer for us all. What do you think?"

I could picture Frank thinking about this. He didn't make choices quickly, I remembered. I motioned to Becky to let me have the phone.

"Frank, Linda here. I'd say it would take us about a month to get everything set up and running smoothly. Then we'd like to start taking a week at home when we wanted to. But one of us would be there all the time. Will this work for you?"

"I don't know. Can I think about it a day or two? I don't know how to make the breakfast part work by myself, and I sure don't know how to decorate the place."

"Sure, think about it. We'd have it all up and running before either of us took a week off. Think about it. And Frank, I had one other idea I'd like to run by you. How about beginning a new tradition. We thought we might plan to have a community Christmas Day celebration there. A pitch-in dinner, decorate a tree, sing some carols, and send everyone home with leftovers. How does that sound to you?"

"Now, that idea I like. So many of us just kind of skip Christmas for lack of family. This would give everybody something to look forward to, and I'd even furnish the turkey, if Tubby will cook it for us."

"I'm excited about this idea. Becky and I could plan the menu and prepare some of it and ask other people to bring the rest. I think it would be great fun."

"Okay. This idea helps me decide. Let's try it the way you guys have thought of. If it doesn't work, we'll just change how we do it. When can you get here?"

Becky waved for the phone now. "We'll be there the day after Thanksgiving. That'll give us plenty of time to get things in order and plan a grand opening on Christmas Day. How's that?"

"That sounds good. Now, remember I don't have much of a budget."

"We have enough stuff from our houses to do the decorating, and Linda has already thought about inexpensive ways to offer a light breakfast each morning. I think you'll increase your business, once people discover you. And we'll work on getting people to discover you. We'll talk about that when we get there."

"Good. I'll watch for you the day after Thanksgiving, and you just tell me what you need from me when you get here. I'll have your living quarters ready by then."

"Yipee! We'll be there and rarin' to go. Thanks, Frank."

I yelled from across the room, "You won't be sorry, Frank, I promise. See you soon."

We returned to the kitchen just as the dishes were finished—good timing. It was easy enough for the others to know Frank's answer by looking at our happy faces.

We spent the time before Thanksgiving packing and planning. I promised the doctor to get lots of exercise—I didn't have to tell him how—and to be diligent about my medication and doctor appointments. Becky promised Sonya to buy one of those old folks pill dispensers and actually use it, to get her daily exercise—I wasn't so sure about the daily part—and to come home often.

Both families and Doug and Jake were coming to my house for Thanksgiving, and we planned to leave the following day. The guys were bringing a small rental truck, and Becky and I would follow them in our own cars. It would be a joyous caravan.

Thanksgiving dinner was the best in years. I cooked a huge turkey and made the dressing. Mandy brought sweet potatoes and her special beets. Sonya brought cranberry salad and green beans. Becky, of course, brought chocolate—tons of chocolate. No pumpkin at our feast no matter what the tradition. Doug and Jake arrived with an abundant supply of wine and in time to have a long conversation with Ralph. When the buzzer went off, signaling the turkey was ready, Jake helped me in the kitchen with the last minute things.

At the table, I clanged on my wine glass to get everyone's attention. "I'd like to propose a toast." All eyes were on me. I had to get this just right. No irreverent humor, I reminded myself. "To the very best children and grandchildren on earth. People who don't put themselves first and who share in the joy of this new endeavor. To Becky, the best friend in the whole world. Sassy, spontaneous, problematic, and wonderful." I turned toward Doug and Jake. "And to our new friends and our new life. For all the people at this table, I am thankful." All wine glasses lifted together, and each of us said our own private thank yous. This would be one of those moments crystallized in my memory.

The next afternoon, we loaded up and drove to Frank's Place. I enjoyed having several hours of time alone on the drive. It was hard to absorb all the changes in my life over the last three months. Not just a renewed relationship with Mandy, but a new kind of relationship. I was proud at a level only mothers can be. So many new friends in Eddyville and the new venture at Frank's Place to relieve the boredom that happens after a few years of retirement. And enough of a health scare to make me take better care of myself. Of course, there was Jake. Now that was an opportunity I had never even considered. It was enough to make a senior giddy.

We drove into the parking lot just as it was getting dark, but Frank had lights on everywhere. As the four of us got out of our vehicles and stretched, Frank came out to greet us. His expression reflected the same anticipation and excitement that I had been feeling on the drive here.

"I was beginning to wonder when you'd get here. Come in and get some coffee before I show you your new quarters." Frank took the overnight bag I had and then did the same for Becky. We trooped inside and stood around stretching our cramped muscles. Frank must have spent some time cleaning—everything in the lobby was sparkling clean and the old musty smell was gone.

Becky and I were dying to see our quarters. "Let's go put these bags in our rooms and then have some coffee." I simply could not wait to see where we would be living.

Everyone went up the steps at the back of the lobby, single file. The exercise felt good after several hours in the car. We made our way to the end of the hallway where there was an L-wing to the motel. Frank unlocked a doorway that I did not remember being at the end of the hall. He must have put that in for our privacy, complete with a deadbolt lock.

When Becky and I walked through the door, we gasped in surprise. Frank had taken three of the larger rooms and turned them into an apartment for us. We entered a large living area and what had been a bathroom was now a small efficiency kitchen. On either side of this room, Becky and I had our own private bedroom and bathroom. And everything was sparkling clean.

"Frank, how did you manage to make this so perfect? Even the windows have been washed!" I was impressed.

"Well, for some reason, the deputy particularly wanted to wash the windows. I didn't get that, but he said the two of you would understand." He looked at us in hopes of an explanation.

Becky and I looked at each other, wide-eyed, and shrugged. She threw up her hands and responded, "I can't imagine what he was talking about."

"Me either. But the windows look great, and there's so much light. I may ask the deputy to go wash the windows at my house in Millerton."

After we put our bags in the bedrooms and looked around, we returned to the lobby. Jake and Doug volunteered to take the truck to Doug's house and come back the next day to unload it. We walked out with them to say goodnight and Frank chose not to follow.

When we went back inside a few minutes later, Frank explained the food out on a table in the lobby. "Lydia and Mamie and Tubby put this together. They knew you'd be too tired to cook when you got here."

"I think I have died and gone to heaven. Makes me wonder why we even had to think about whether to come here." I filled a Dixie plate as I talked.

Becky and Frank were right behind me, and soon we sat together in lobby chairs eating to our stomachs' content.

Becky, the decorator, kicked in. "Frank, our quarters are just great. And I think I can do some things in the lobby that you'll like without spending a dime. Linda already figured out how to offer some breakfast to guests with very little trouble or expense."

He looked up, with fork poised in the air. "Really? The breakfast thing has always been a problem. And I have no idea what needs to be done in the lobby. I think this is going to be a good partnership." He looked as close to happy as I had ever seen him.

"I do too. Give Becky and me a week, and we'll have this place humming. You may have to tell us when we're about to overdo it."

"Not a chance of that." I was glad Frank was secure in this arrangement.

After supper, we excused ourselves and went 'home'. Once in our quarters, we could not contain our comments.

"They scraped and cleaned and polished everything in here. And I thought I'd lose it when Frank said the deputy wanted to clean the windows. We have to go say hello and thank you—for the windows and for his discretion." I walked around the apartment as I talked.

Becky did a visual inspection from the couch. "This is a nice arrangement. And we both have privacy in our bedrooms. Not that we'll need that, of course." Her crooked grin couldn't be contained.

"Oh, no. Of course not." I turned to smile at her. "But we might need to talk about that as it applies to our individual 'exercise' plans." We dissolved into another of our laughing fits.

Getting ready for bed later, I couldn't help wondering what the future would hold. Here we were—two feisty boomers on the loose in a new place with new 'boyfriends' and only the Lord in Heaven knew what that would mean.